JOURNEY TO A NEW BEGINNING

Higher Ways Series Book 3

Small Pond Press
Box 637 Blackfalds
Alberta Canada
T0M 0J0

smallpond@telus.net

First Edition
Published by Small Pond Press

Arise, shine: for thy light is come,
and the glory of the Lord is risen upon thee.
For behold, the darkness shall cover the earth,
and gross darkness the people;
but the Lord shall arise upon thee,
and his glory shall be seen upon thee.

Isaiah 60:1,2 King James Version

Chapter One

The thunder of horse's hooves made the hay loft where Ulhrik lay shake. He raised himself up and peered through the slats of the wall into the yard below. He held his breath when he saw the farmer raise the pitchfork he held in one hand. The other rested on a boy's shoulder as the mounted soldiers charged into the small farmyard. Ulhrik did not move when the men dismounted and stood at silent attention while their captain spurred his horse into the barn, then charged back and peered down at the farmer and the boy. He circled them several times and knocked the pitchfork from the man's hand before dismounting. He drew his sword and confronted the farmer. Ulhrik could hear his guttural voice clearly.

"We are looking for Prince Eghan Lhin. If you have seen him, speak now, or suffer loss."

"I have seen no prince," the man replied.

The captain glared at him, then snorted and signaled his men. The farmer did not move but Ulhrik could see the tension in his back as they ransacked the house and barn. Ulhrik buried himself in the hay and held his breath when he heard footsteps ascending the ladder to the loft. He let it out again when the ladder creaked as the soldier descended. Taking care not to make a sound as he shifted beneath the hay, he pulled himself up and peered back out into the yard. The captain stood only inches from the farmer's face.

"I ask you once more, have you seen the prince?" Ulhrik prayed the man's voice would remain steady.

"And I tell you again, I have not," the farmer stated firmly.

The captain raised his sword and struck him with its hilt, then mounted and led his men back onto the road. The farmer remained on the ground as they thundered by, then stood slowly to his feet. He wiped the blood from his forehead but as he turned toward the barn Ulrick saw that a smile played on his lips. He looked down at the boy and winked.

When the soldiers vanished into a plume of dust, Ulhrik climbed down, meeting the man and boy as they ran into the barn. They forked a pile of foul straw away and dropped to their knees to remove the floor boards.

"It is not a prince we harbor, but a king," the farmer said as the two hidden beneath crawled out, coughing and blinking into the dim light.

"God reward you for your faithfulness, my friend," Ulhrik said as he helped Eghan and Latham stand.

The farmer nodded at him and bowed to Eghan. "I

am honored to have you here, but I can offer you little."

"A chance to rest for a time is all that is needed." Ulhrik said as he and Latham helped Eghan walk toward the house. When Eghan stumbled and sank down, throwing Ulhrik off balance, the husky farmer scooped his young king into his arms as though he were a child and entered his home.

Eghan woke, sensing a blaze of fire as his eyes flickered open and he jerked fully awake. Fear coursed through him with the memory of the red-hot iron Ulhrik had used to sear his arm. But that was days ago. Here, this fire was contained in a small hearth. Latham lay at his side, stretched out on a mat on the floor. A small boy stood by the fire, staring. When Eghan lowered himself back onto his straw pallet, the boy darted out the door. A moment later Ulhrik entered, nudged Latham awake with the toe of his boot and stood over their king.

"There will be a hearty breakfast for you in a few moments, Sire." He slipped his arm under Eghan's shoulders and helped him sit up.

"We should not stay. We have put these people in danger of losing their property, if not their very lives. We must leave before we bring more trouble upon them."

A deep voice boomed from the doorway. "Do not fret about us, Sire. After the ransacking those soldiers did to this place four days ago, they won't be back, at least not for a while."

Eghan stared at the man's massive form, filling the doorway. His clothes were ragged but his broad face, framed by a mass of curly brown hair, beamed with good nature.

"Four days?" He looked at Ulhrik.

The old man nodded. "You were delirious for a time." He touched Eghan's forehead. "But the fever has broken now."

The farmer approached with a bowl and spoon. "Eat, my lord, and your strength will return."

Eghan took the bowl. "I thank you for your loyalty. Your name?"

"Isham, Sire."

Eghan glanced at the boy peeping out from behind the man. "And your son?"

The farmer reached back and grasped the boy's shirt, pulling him before them. "This little heap of bones is my brother's son, Tobhin, Sire."

The small boy grinned at him so impishly, Eghan forced a smile. Then the room began to spin. In an instant, Ulhrik and Latham were upon him. He leaned back and closed his eyes.

"Don't exert yourself, Sire." Ulhrik's voice was thick with concern.

Eghan opened his eyes. "Bring me some water, Latham." The cold drink revived him. Isham placed the dish of thick porridge in his lap again and promised meat for their dinner. Eghan thought to offer the man a reward but did not allow the words out of his mouth. How could he reward anyone? He had no money, no position, not even a home. He was more destitute than this farmer. He ate the porridge and felt strengthened by it, but did not move from the pallet.

For the next week the routine was the same. The farmer and his nephew went about their chores while their king ate and slept, his servants hovering over him. On the eighth day, Isham reported that another band of soldiers had moved across his land. That night Ulhrik forced Eghan to rise and eat at the table with them.

"We must plan, Sire. When you are strong enough, we must be on our way."

"On our way where, Ulhrik?" Eghan's own voice sounded thin and flat in his ears.

"The world is larger than you imagine," Ulhrik said. "It encompasses much more than the Valley of Lhin and the Alinga Territories."

"And how are we to make our way in it -- a maimed king, an old man and a stable boy?"

"We will trust the One True God, as we have done in the past."

"That does not seem to have been to our benefit thus far." Eghan saw Ulhrik's eye's narrow at the bitter edge to his voice. He was surprised but relieved that the old man chose to ignore it.

"There is a country, small, but prosperous and well fortified," Ulhrik said, "at the edge of the sea. I believe it will afford us a safe refuge, for now."

Isham's voice chimed in. "The realm called Brimladin. Yes, it is a fine land, well ruled. Its people are skilled at reaping the bounty of the sea." Isham took a step toward them and his eyes shone. "It is a wondrous thing to behold, that sea; a body of water so vast you cannot see an end to it."

Eghan did not respond. He ate the rest of his meal in silence and returned to his pallet.

Ulhrik and Isham remained sitting at the rough table. It was some time before Eghan heard their hushed voices.

"He is wounded as much in his spirit as in his body, I fear." Isham's soft statement made Ulhrik sigh.

"He needs healing in both, my friend."

Isham was quiet for a time, then Eghan heard the sound of a wooden bowl being pushed across the table.

"You will need a guide to Brimladin," the farmer said. "The roads are dangerous, more so now, with Damon's soldiers searching for him. You will have to travel overland. It will take several weeks and it will be a hard journey."

Ulhrik sighed again. "The King is not strong enough to ride, and I fear the boy and I are not strong enough to pull a cart all the way to the sea. Do you know of someone we could trust, someone with a small wagon perhaps?"

Isham did not respond immediately. Eghan heard

the crackling of wood in the hearth. When the farmer spoke again his voice had the ring of determination.

"You can trust me. I will go with you."

"A gracious offer, my friend," Ulhrik said. "But we cannot ask you to leave your farm, your family."

"My wife died in childbirth a year ago." Eghan heard the ring of sorrow in his voice as the man continued. "Since then I have had little heart for the farm work. My brother sent Tobhin to try to keep me going, and he has been a Godsend, but I know he misses his own family." The farmer's bench creaked. "I will arrange to leave my holdings in my brother's care. You will need a strong man to get you to the city of Brimladin Ula."

"Do you know the place well?" Ulhrik asked.

"I traveled far and wide when I was young and restless. And my wife's family lives there. If we can find them, I believe we can depend on them for some help when we arrive."

"Then you too are a Godsend, Isham."

The next day, Isham and his nephew left at first light, driving four cows before them. The farmer returned alone, driving a small wagon with a rounded frame covered with faded yellow cloth. The horse looked very old. The day after that, Eghan found himself peering out under the flapping edge of a ragged tarp. As he watched the small farm grow smaller behind them, he thought to pray, but did not. He scratched at the rough cloth of his tunic and breeches and thought of the soft garments and leather boots hidden with his father's sword, beneath him. He had disguised himself this way before and reveled in the adventure. Now he regarded himself and knew this was no disguise. This was who he was -- a beggar with a useless right arm and not enough strength to walk a mile. They would sell his fine clothing and boots as soon as it appeared safe to do so. Perhaps they would even have to sell his father’s sword.

As his thoughts darkened, Eghan pulled back from the opening. Let the land go by unheeded, he thought. It is no longer any of my concern. At that moment, the tarp flew up and Latham boosted himself up onto the back of the wagon, letting his legs dangle from the backboard. His face brightened. "Well, we're on our way, Sire!"

"Do not call me Sire, Latham." Eghan's voice sounded harsher than he intended. "It will be too dangerous now," he said more softly.

The boy dropped his head. "Yes, my....I mean no...I mean..." he sighed. "It's goin' to take some gettin' used to, is all."

Eghan pulled a blanket over himself and turned away. He heard Latham sigh again and shifted to face the road just as the cart lurched into the ditch and back up into a darkly shaded wood. He sat up when the blanket that separated them from Ulhrik and Isham moved. Ulhrik peered over his shoulder.

"That will be the last bit of road we'll see for some time," he said. "Pray God will help us find a clear path to the sea."

Eghan lay down again, closed his eyes and fell into a restless sleep. He dreamed of the snake-like creature again. It hissed and writhed about him, growing into a massive dragon that made him cower. He jerked awake several times, staring at the roof until the swaying of the wagon put him to sleep again.

Chapter Two

If it hadn't been unseemly, Nara would have craned her neck out the window of the carriage to better see the town through which they were traveling. What she could see impressed her as the carriage rolled swiftly down narrow streets, over well-swept cobblestones. The city was large, reasonably clean and bustling with activity.

Brynna gasped and clutched her arm. "Oh, my lady, look!"

Nara leaned over her, then called for the driver to stop as they reached the crest of a hill. They stepped out and around the carriage to better see what was before them. Nara followed the wide road with her eyes as it descended again into the thick of the city and made its way straight toward the castle on a higher hill opposite where they stood. The edifice gleamed white in the morning sun, the blue of the sea an ever-shifting backdrop to its splendor.

"Perhaps we should find an inn, m'lady?" Brynna spoke softly. "So you can change into your best dress?"

"And if I wear my best dress on arrival, what will I wear when I am presented to the king, Brynna?" Nara looked down at the plain frock and faded cape she wore and sighed. "No. I'm afraid there is nothing for it but to appear as the country bumpkin I am." She stared at the castle for another moment, then motioned to her hand-maid and climbed back into the carriage.

As it began to move she pondered what Gage had told her about the family she was about to meet. It seemed King Delmar was known for his shrewd but fair dealings with his allies and foes alike. He had assumed the throne when still a teenager, after the death of his father who had been deeply mourned by the Brimleish. The son was not as greatly loved, Gage had said, but well respected. He lived in the grand castle that loomed before them with the queen mother, two younger brothers and the one sister who was about to have her coming out ball. Burke had been able to find out little more about them.

Nara took in a deep breath as the carriage clattered over the cobblestones and came to a stop before a high iron gate. A guardsman peered in at them as her driver handed him the invitation. Then Nara heard a shout and the gate opened. The carriage rattled over an arched bridge across a wide mote fed by the sea. The aqua flow rose and fell with a mesmerizing movement. Nara pulled her eyes away from it and said a quick prayer. She took another deep breath as they slowed and entered an enormous courtyard.

The large wooden doors of the castle stood open before them. A long line of servants bowed as she stepped from the carriage, Brynna at her heels. Nara smiled and stepped forward just as an older woman appeared in the doorway. She stood straight with the bearing of a queen, her hands clasped quietly in front of her glimmering gown, but she too was smiling. As Nara approached, the woman came toward her with her hands extended.

"Welcome, my dear," she said. "I am Aerwyna, queen mother to King Delmar. Welcome to Brimladin Ula, and to our home."

Nara stared, then recovered herself quickly and curtsied. "It is an honor to meet you, Queen Aerwyna."

The woman took her hands. "And it is a delight to me that you are here. Come, you must be weary after such a long journey." She led her into the castle, through an enormous marble entry, down a wide corridor and up a spiraling stairway made of more gleaming white stone.

Nara was painfully aware of the six men who trooped after her. She knew Gage had given them strict instructions to never leave her side and she also knew they would take that order seriously but she wished there was some way to make them keep their distance. She hoped their presence would not be taken as an insult by her hosts.

Nara almost gasped when the queen mother

opened the doors into a large bright room lavishly decorated and hung with tapestries. A huge bouquet of flowers sat on a gleaming table, a bowl of fresh fruit beside it.

"I hope you won't mind being in the older section of our home, Queen Nara. It will be quieter here and the view is better. But these rooms can be a bit drafty at times, so if you are uncomfortable in any way please let me know and we will find something else for you."

"I'm sure this will be fine, your Grace."

The queen mother smiled again. "Please, call me Aerwyna. And may I address you by your given name?"

Nara smiled back at the warmth in the woman's eyes. "Of course, please do."

Aerwyna nodded. "Good. My chambers are just down the hall to the right, Nara. If you need anything at all, call for a servant or ..." she glanced at the men standing at the door... "send one of your own."

When she turned back her smile told Nara that she understood and had not taken offense.

"I've ordered some refreshments sent up for you. Rest now. My son will receive you at the banquet this evening."

As the doors closed softly Nara looked at Brynna and they both giggled.

"I feel like we've stepped into a magical place, my lady," Brynna said.

Nara stepped onto the balcony that afforded her a

wide view of the city and the sea beyond. She breathed in the moist air and felt refreshed. Perhaps Burke was right. Her time here would be a welcome respite from the worries of rebuilding her own kingdom. She wished Eghan could be at her side. *He would love this place,* she thought. The disturbing dread she had felt before leaving Alinga Territory lingered and Nara wondered as she peered out at the sea, if it had been a true premonition that something dreadful had happened, or was about to happen, in the Valley of Lhin.

She shook herself and asked Brynna to prepare her a hot bath as she tried to banish the gloomy thoughts of Eghan and his kingdom. She had to think of her own. The banquet tonight could prove to be of great consequence to her people. *And perhaps,* Nara thought, *even to my own future.*

When the doors swung open to the banquet hall Nara heard Brynna's soft gasp. The walls were trimmed with gold and green, the beams high and sweeping. To one side long tables were laden with food of every kind, including a large sculpture of a leaping sea creature that appeared to be made of ice. The room was full of men and women dressed in the finest of fashion.

Nara smoothed the front of her gown, painfully aware that it was not nearly as grand as those she saw around her. She heard her name being announced, raised her chin and stepped forward. A young man of about her own age approached. He was slim and almost seemed to float across the gleaming floor. His blue eyes studied her and his long blond hair fell in a wave as he gave a quick bow, introduced himself and offered his arm.

"I am Prince Muirgheal, my lady, second son of the late King Kinreig and brother of King Delmar. I am pleased to escort you."

Nara nodded her thanks, rested her hand on his arm and let him lead her forward. The crowd parted as they went, a hush falling that allowed her to hear some of the whispers as all eyes followed her.

Muirgheal bent his head toward her, his blond hair spilling over his shoulder as he said softly, "Don't be anxious, Queen Nara. Most here are friendly. My brother frowns a lot but he is not the hard heart he seems."

Nara let out her breath and nodded again. She hoped she would not be so tongue-tied when she stood before the king.

King Delmar sat on a raised dais, his right hand holding a golden scepter as the guests streamed by and bowed before him. To most he gave a slight nod. Every now and then he spoke a word or two to the one before him. He appeared to be taller than his brother, with a strong jaw and the same thick yellow hair but his was bound behind his neck. His satin robes were rich and he wore a jeweled crown on his head.

Nara moved slowly forward on Murigheal's arm. At last she heard her name called. She curtsied deeply then stood and began to turn to follow those who had been presented before her. But the king spoke.

"Welcome to the court of Brimladin Ula, Queen Nara Alingar."

"It is my honor to be here, King Delmar."

He gave her a slight smile. "And I would be honored if you would join me at the banquet table. There are important matters I wish to discuss with you."

Nara smiled back and ducked her head. "Of course, Your Majesty." She glanced at Queen Aerwyna, smiling at the king's side. The woman gave her a small nod as her smile widened.

Muirgheal stepped to her side again and led her away, introducing her quietly to others who had moved aside. Nara noted that some greeted her with warmth in their eyes, some with open curiosity and some with wariness. A few of the younger women seemed almost hostile. The prince kept up a steady banter, entertaining her with his comments on some of the guests.

When all had been presented the king stood. A trumpet sounded briefly and the crowd parted, all eyes turning toward the doors. A young woman dressed in a sparkling blue gown glided toward the king. Her yellow hair was gathered up but still hung to her shoulders in flowing curls. Even from a distance Nara could tell she had the family's startling blue eyes. The princess smiled and nodded as she floated past the men and women watching her. Her grace was evident in that smile and Nara knew just by looking at her face that she would like this young woman.

When the girl reached the king she curtsied deeply. King Delmar's face beamed with approval. He took her hand and led her up onto the dais, turning to the audience. "Honored guests, it is my privilege to present my sister, Princess Talwynn Ul."

The crowd erupted with applause. Two courtiers approached from either side, bowed and then placed a gleaming tiara on the girl's head. The crowd erupted again and music was struck.

The king raised his voice to be heard. "I invite you to celebrate with us on this happy occasion. Eat, dance, enjoy the bounty of our land." He took his sister's hand again and they moved through the parting audience toward the long tables already laden with food. Muirgheal took Nara's elbow and led her immediately after them.

Before the king sat he turned to Nara. "Queen Nara, may I present my sister, Princess Talwynn." Nara smiled and bowed her head, surprised when the girl took another step and embraced her, kissing her on both cheeks.

"Welcome, Queen Nara. I hope we will become friends and ..." her eyes flicked to Muirgheal's face and gave him an impish grin ... "perhaps more, in the days ahead."

Nara did not have the chance to reply as the prince took her arm and led her to a chair beside the king. He clapped his hands and signaled the maids behind them to begin serving.

"I trust your journey was not too arduous?"

The intensity of the king's blue eyes made Nara a bit uneasy but she answered quickly. "Not overly so, Your Highness, though the roads between our two kingdoms are rather rough."

He nodded. "Yes. A detail we will have to rectify in the future. Perhaps."

"I am sure my people would be pleased to share the burden of that cost." She paused. "Were it to be necessary."

"I have heard there has been much restoration going on in the Alinga Territory. Is that not taxing your treasury?"

"I admit it is, yes, but my people have been unrelenting and labor without much pay to do the work needed."

A large platter of seafood was set before them and Nara was staring at it, wondering what to choose when an arm suddenly reached between them and a voice from behind her made her jump. "Try this one." The hand gripped a pair of wooden tongs and lifted a large chunk of some kind of fish onto her plate.

Nara shifted and turned to see a young man dressed in a plain brown tunic. If he had not been almost a double of the brother she had already met, she would have thought him a servant.

"Sit down, Brimwell." The king's voice showed his irritation. "And mind your manners."

The young man winked at Nara and withdrew his arm. Before she could speak he had pulled out the chair beside her, which Muirgheal had just vacated, and sat down, leaning toward her conspiratorially as he said in a loud stage whisper. "My brother is overly concerned about table manners, my lady, so don't slurp your soup."

She tried to hide a grin as Talwynn giggled and the king sighed. This then, was the youngest brother. His hair was the same color but shorter and wilder, framing his angular face in curls. His eyes were like the king's but larger and much more friendly.

"I hope you'll like that," he said, pointing to the fish on her plate. "It's one of my favorites. They catch it right here in the bay. I've caught a few myself. They give a good fight for their size."

"If you will stop babbling perhaps she'll have a chance to try it, little brother."

Brimwell rolled his eyes, scooped a large portion of the fish onto his own plate and quickly forked a sizeable chunk into his mouth. Nara almost laughed out loud at the mischievous twinkle in his eyes as he smacked his lips. She did laugh out loud a number of times as the meal went on. Brimwell's wit was quick, and all the more so as Muirgheal, who had seated himself beside him, joined in. She tried to quell her laughter for the sake of the king, who seemed increasingly unamused at his younger brothers' banter and his sister's giggling.

When they were finished eating the king stood

and bowed toward her. "Perhaps tomorrow morning you would join me for a walk in the gardens, Queen Nara? There we can talk without the distractions that have kept us from serious conversation this evening." He gave his brothers a withering glance.

Nara nodded. "I would be honored, Your Highness."

He bowed again and took his leave. As Nara turned back to the other two brothers she caught a look passing between them but they both dropped their eyes and said nothing.

Then Brimwell sprang to his feet. "Do you dance, Queen Nara?"

"Dance? Well, I ..."

Muirgheal stood up as well. "There are no better minstrels than those in the court of Brimladin Ula."

"I'm afraid I would not know the steps."

"Then we .." the brothers' voices blended, "... will teach you,"

Brimwell took her elbow and lifted her from the chair. Muirgheal stepped quickly to her side. Talwynn leaped to her feet, clapping her hands. She wiggled between her brothers and took Nara's arm, entwining it with her own. "My brothers are splendid dancers," she said.

Within moments Nara found herself being spun across the floor in the midst of many others. Both brothers were light on their feet and excellent teachers. It did not take Nara long to catch the way of the dances and between the two young men she barely had a moment to breathe before she was swept away again. She noticed Talwynn was also kept spinning by a series of ardent admirers.

After a particularly fast reel, Nara disengaged herself from Brimwell's grasp and sank down on a chair, panting. The prince squatted at her feet and Talwynn plopped down in a chair beside her.

"I hope they haven't worn you out, my lady," Talwynn said, her blue eyes dancing.

Nara took a deep breath. "I must say it has been a delight, Princess Talwynn. I haven't danced like this in ... well, ever. But I am rather tired now, yes."

Brimwell stood and stepped back. "Of course. Will you allow me to escort you to your chambers?"

"Or I?" Muirgheal stepped up quickly and Talwynn giggled.

"That is not necessary." Nara waved at her guards who lingered near the entry. "I always have an escort."

"Yes," Muirgheal said. "So we have noticed." Nara wondered at the look he gave his brother before bowing deeply. He lifted his head and smiled at her. "Good night, then."

Brimwell did the same, with a wink, leaving Nara to summon Brynna and make her way to her bedchamber.

As Brynna helped her out of her gown the girl chatted on about how well she and the other servants were treated. "This certainly isn't what I expected, m'lady."

"What do you mean, Brynna?"

The girl cocked her head. "Well, I'm not sure what I expected really, but it wasn't this. This place truly is magical. The princess is so lovely and gracious, and her brothers! Oh my!" Her hand flew to her mouth and she giggled. "I overheard gossip that the king will ..." She stopped suddenly.

Nara turned to face her. "The king will what?"

Brynna dropped her eyes. "Well, m'lady, they said the king is determined to marry one of them off and foist the other one off as a knight to our court." She giggled again. "They obviously don't know that we don't yet have a court on which to foist him."

"Nor that I am not looking for a husband."

"But they are charming, are they not, m'lady?"

"Charm is not the only characteristic needed in a husband, Brynna, especially one that must help to rule a realm."

"No m'lady," she agreed as she swept the dress up. "But I imagine it wouldn't hurt."

Nara grinned and shook a finger at her. "I hope you did not contribute to the gossip, my girl."

Brynna shook her head and was suddenly serious. "Oh my, no, m'lady. I would never betray your trust in that way."

Nara smiled. "Good. Now find your own bed." She yawned. "I am weary beyond speech."

Brynna curtsied and left her. As Nara pulled the thick quilts up to her chin and lay her head on the soft pillow, her mind was still filled with the glittering gowns, the laughter and music, and the smiling eyes of the two handsome princes. She had almost nodded off before realizing she should pray again for Eghan and his kingdom and the safety of her own. She wondered if he was sleeping as comfortably as she this night.

Chapter Three

Eghan heard the music and lifted his head to peer through the flapping fabric that covered the wagon. He saw firelight flickering through the trees. The wagon stopped and Latham was about to leap out when Isham's shaggy head popped through the partition.

"Stay hidden," he said. "I will find out who these people are."

Eghan slipped back down into the blankets and waited. He heard Latham slip out but did not try to stop him. It seemed a long time before the flap flew up and the boy grinned at him.

"Gypsies," he said. "They've invited us to share their fire, Sire, at least for the night. Their pots smell wonderful, they do. D'ye think they'll feed us too? They seems quite happy to have us here."

"Hoping to rob us blind, no doubt," Ulhrik said as he came to the wagon and peered in at them. "You're sure the sword is well hidden, Latham?"

The boy's eyes widened as he nodded. "Yes, m'lord."

Ulhrik nodded and reached to help Eghan

from the wagon. "Then we will join them, for the time being, but keep your eyes open and say nothing." He looked down his nose at Latham. "Nothing at all."

The music stopped as the small group made their way toward the fire at the center of the camp. A large man with long black hair hanging across his shoulders in braids came toward them. He was dressed in flamboyant clothing, a green shirt with billowing sleeves and a red sash around his waist. The sash held a dagger whose tip curved out from under it. His smile gleamed in the firelight. Eghan thought he saw a glint of gold in one of the man's teeth.

"Welcome, travelers," he said. "I am Balor Engre, leader of this happy band." He waved his hand toward the circle of men, women and children who now stood silently staring at them. Balor stopped a few paces from them. Eghan noticed his dark eyes did not stop moving over each of them. "Are you traveling far, my friends?"

Ulhrik's answer was evasive. "Only as far as need be."

Balor's mouth jerked into a grin as his eyes flicked to Eghan. "And perhaps yours is a journey of necessity, yes?"

"Are not all journeys so?"

The gypsy nodded. "And often laid out for us in the stars. We are all people of destiny, are we not?"

"But the One who controls that destiny is wise."

"One?" Balor's eyebrows rose. "You follow one god then?"

Ulhrik nodded. "The One True God who holds all of our destinies in his hands."

Balor's voice dropped. "In these uncertain times there are places where that name should not be spoken, my friend, if one values his life and the security of his neck."

Ulhrik sighed as he nodded again. "We know that full well."

The gypsy cocked his head and seemed to make a decision. "Then you are indeed welcome among us." His eyes swept over their wagon. "But perhaps you have something, just a small token of friendship, you understand, something that would ease the minds of those who do not so readily accept strangers among us?"

"I think we may have just such a thing," Ulhrik nodded and gave the man a slight bow.

Balor beamed, stepped close and clapped Ulhrick on the back. "Then come, warm yourselves at our fires."

Ulhrik spoke quietly to Latham. The boy nodded and turned back to their wagon as the others moved toward the group of men, women and children. Balor spoke rapidly in a tongue Eghan did not know and the circle of people relaxed. The fiddler took up his bow again and began to play, but more quietly. Wooden stumps were set before them. Eghan was thankful to sink down onto one. Latham appeared again, carrying Eghan's leather boots and some of his clothing. The boy gave Eghan a quick glance as he passed them to Ulhrik and watched him hand them to the gypsy leader.

"These should fetch a good price in any marketplace."

Balor ran his hand over the boots. "Indeed they will." He handed them off to a younger man and spoke quickly again. Eghan watched his fine boots disappear. When he looked back at Balor the gypsy was watching him. His eyes narrowed as they rested on Eghan's cradled arm.

"You have met with some foul play I see?"

Ulhrik did not give Eghan a chance to speak. "Yes. He was attacked some days ago. He is still recovering."

"We have herbs that will help," Balor said. He snapped his fingers and said a few words to a young boy who immediately darted away. He called out a name and an old woman placed a large steaming pot before them and handed Latham a ladle and four rough bowls. She waved her hand at the pot and put her hand to her mouth, giving them a toothless grin. Latham dipped the ladle into the soup and served it up. Eghan let his bowl sit at his feet.

In a few moments another younger woman appeared with a smaller pot. She poured a foul smelling liquid into a tin cup, reached a dirty hand under Eghan's chin and raised his head so he was forced to look into her dark eyes. "Drink. Medicine," she said. Eghan pushed her hand away.

Ulhrik took the cup and thanked her. "He will drink it," he said.

The girl frowned and stepped back.

Ulhrik handed the cup to Eghan. "Drink," he said.

Eghan raised his eyes to Ulhrik's and knew the man would give him no choice. He noticed how the Gypsy leader and the young woman leaned forward, watching. "It could be poison," he said softly.

Ulhrik shook his head. "I see no malice in their eyes."

Eghan raised the cup to his lips but quickly pulled it away. "It smells like manure."

"Perhaps it is." Ulhrik chuckled. "But drinking it will please our hosts and I have no doubt it will help. These people have been making medicines from the earth for generations. I've seen their potions work miracles." He raised Eghan's hand back to his mouth. "Drink it," he said again.

Eghan gulped it down and coughed for several moments. Balor and the young woman laughed and nodded. Eghan reached for the bowl of soup at his feet and spooned some into his mouth to get rid of the taste. He saw the young woman hand Ulhrik a small pouch.

"Mix a healthy pinch in water," she said, "twice a day until he is strong again."

Ulhrik thanked her and handed the bag to Latham. "Put this somewhere safe, " he said.

Latham nodded and glanced at Eghan.

"Shall I hide it, sir?" he asked in a whisper loud enough for Eghan to hear.

Ulhrik gave him a quick nod. Eghan turned away and pretended he had not seen the exchange.

Some time after they had finished eating, the people slowly wandered away to their wagons. Balor invited Ulhrik to drive theirs closer and the old man nodded at Isham. Eghan joined him in the wagon as he urged the horse forward, looking around them as their wagon took up a spot in the gypsy's circle. He breathed in the smoky scent of the gypsies' fires mingled with the smell of spruce and pine trees. It brought back memories of his days living outdoors with his uncle and Nara.

Suddenly very weary, he settled into his bed inside, listening with half an ear to the murmur of Ulhrik and Balor's voices as they continued in conversation. He wondered what the new day would bring. One thing was certain. They were now part of the gypsy's caravan.

****

Damon pulled at his hair as he strode from one side of his chamber to the other, not caring what his generals might think. His soldiers had failed to find the prince and a nagging dread would not leave him. The boy must be found. The best plan was to coerce the prince into standing with him so the Lhinian people believed he had the support of their royal line. His physician's potions would work to secure and enhance the boy's willingness. The alternative of course was to have him killed quietly. Damon punched a fist into the palm of his other hand. They had to find him! As long as the prince was out of his reach his hold on this kingdom was in jeopardy.

And he knew that as long as these people held onto their faith, his schemes would not succeed. He scowled at the soldier waiting by the hearth and stared at the book that had just been handed to him. He cursed, grabbed it up from the table and threw it into the fire. The flames licked at it hungrily.

"The Lhinian king succeeded in spreading the poison of his religion before we managed to take control. We must see that it is eradicated." He raised his head and looked at the generals waiting for his orders. "Totally eradicated. Is that understood?"

The soldiers nodded.

"You know what to do," Damon continued. "Erect a whipping post in every village and see that it is well used. The rabble must be subdued and controlled. And do it quickly. Our energies need to be focused on building our army. We must be ready to invade before the Alingans have a chance to mobilize." He waved his hand in impatience and bellowed. "Go!"

One man remained, waiting. Damon waved him close after the others had gone. "Have you broken him yet?"

"No, my lord. The man still refuses to speak."

Damon snorted. "Then perhaps he needs the touch of a master."

The man bowed and followed as the Duke headed for the subterranean reaches of the castle.

Khalwyd groaned and tried to shift his position, but the shackles on his wrists and ankles held him tight and prevented much movement. It felt like every joint in his body was out of place. He was sure he had at least two broken ribs. One eye was swollen shut and dried blood caked the corners of his swollen mouth. He thought his jaw might be broken and he wondered how much more he could take. But he knew he had to keep focused on staying silent. Eghan's life could depend on that silence and Khalwyd would never betray his long-ago oath to protect the House of Lhin to his dying breath. He turned his head at the sound of heavy footsteps and prayed for the strength to endure what was to come.

Damon held the torch so close to Khalwyd's face he heard the hairs in his beard sizzle. The man smirked at him.

"I am pleased to see you are awake, Khalwyd of Stohl. We have something to discuss." He waved to a soldier and the shackles on Khalwyd's wrists were removed. He was prodded to a sitting position as the shackles on his ankles fell away. Then two men grabbed his arms and dragged him to the center of the cell where they fastened single shackles to each of his wrists. These were attached to two chains which the soldiers fed through iron rings embedded in a low beam. Then they pulled until Khalwyd's feet were dangling just off the floor. He moaned as his body was stretched to its full length.

He heard the hiss of the whip as Damon let it play over the straw-strewn floor. Then he heard it crack as Damon brought it up and flicked it high in the air. Its tip snapped above Khalwyd's ear.

"Where is Prince Eghan?"

Khalwyd turned his head so he could look into the man's face from his one open eye and spoke calmly. "He is no longer a prince. He is a king."

Damon's harsh laughter echoed from the stone walls. "A boy king with no kingdom."

"If he is of no significance why bother trying to find him?"

Damon leaned forward. "Where has he gone?"

Khalwyd stared into his eyes and attempted to smile. "He has the protection of our God, Damon. You cannot reach him unless our God ordains it."

"Look around you, guardian. It appears your God has ordained that you be left out of this grand plan you speak of." He bellowed in Khalwyd's face. "I rule the Valley of Lhin now, Khalwyd of Stohl. You would be wise to align yourself with me, not with a maimed fugitive king and his powerless god."

Guardian, Khalwyd thought. *Yes. That is what I am. What I will always be.* "Never" he said. "I will serve the house of Lhin and the One True God to my dying breath."

"As you wish," Damon growled, moved around

behind him and flicked the whip high. Khalwyd screamed when it struck but clenched his jaw and said nothing more.

When the whip failed to loosen his tongue, Damon tried a different tack. "Your silence will earn you only pain, Khalwyd. The House of Lhin has already been destroyed." His voice was cajoling now, trying to sound so reasonable. "There is no one left who can save you. So save yourself." The voice dropped to a whisper. "Tell me. No one will ever know. Tell me and I will reward you. Where is the prince?"

"He is no prince," Khalwyd repeated. "Eghan Lhin is my king."

The whip whistled as it struck again and again.

Khalwyd closed his eyes and prayed. When he passed out, they woke him, throwing foul water into his face and over his body. The light of the torch cast a menacing beam that gleamed in the liquid as it coursed down the stone walls around them. Khalwyd tried to focus on it, tried to pray again, as the long night continued.

Chapter Four

Roses and a myriad of other flowers waved in a soft breeze as Nara and Brynna walked along the wide garden paths.

"Wouldn't it be wonderful to have such a place at home?" Nara bent down to smell a rose that looked like it had just bloomed.

"It would indeed, m'lady," Brynna answered.

"Perhaps we could borrow a Brimleish gardener and take him back with us."

"That could be arranged."

Brynna jumped back as Nara whirled around to find the king standing close behind her. She and Brynna fell into a deep curtsy.

The king took Nara's hand and raised her up. "We would be happy to share the skills of any of our household with yours, Queen Nara." He didn't smile, but his eyes didn't look quite as intense as they had the night before.

Nara did smile. "Thank you, Your Majesty," she said and curtsied again.

He waved one hand toward the path and took her elbow in the other. "Shall we?"

She nodded and stepped into place beside him, Brynna following a few paces behind.

"Did you enjoy yourself last night?" the king asked. "I noticed my brothers kept you on your feet."

Nara chuckled. "Yes, indeed they did. And yes, I did enjoy myself."

"Good." Delmar's mouth turned up only briefly. They walked in silence for a moment. Then the king stopped and faced her.

"I am not a man who is accustomed to small talk, Queen Nara, and since you have no father or brothers to speak to, I will come to the point quickly. My kingdom is rich in many things but we are lacking the kind of ore needed to fashion the tools and weapons we need - the kind of ore in your Alingan mines. We would seek trade and an alliance with your kingdom as soon as it can be arranged. So, which of my brothers do you prefer?"

"Prefer, Your Majesty?"

"I realize they are both quite immature in some ways but I can assure you they are both intelligent and have been trained in leadership and the protocols of court. Either one would be capable of being your ...." He cocked his head and studied her, then gave a quick nod. "I would think Brimwell would suit you. He is quite fond of ... well, shall we say, the more down to earth things of this world."

Nara realized her mouth had fallen open and she was staring at the king. She gave her head a shake.

"I am rather taken aback, King Delmar. I don't know how you have come to the conclusion that I came here seeking a husband, but ..."

"Come, come, my dear. Surely you did not think our invitation was purely a courtesy? I certainly did not think your appearance here was only to attend my sister's coming out ball. I would have thought you would realize an alliance would be of great benefit to you. Our army is well trained and would of course be at your disposal should it be needed. And if the rumors I hear are true, that may be sooner than any of us would wish. I am sure you will agree, the world is not as secure a place as it once was. In return for your ore we would also offer a portion of the many and varied goods that pour into our country from across the sea. My people are also skilled at harvesting its bounty. I think you will find the arrangement quite generous."

"And what does Brimwell think of such an arrangement?"

"Brimwell, or Muirgheal, will do as they are told, for the good of their country." The king's voice had a harsh edge that made Nara frown.

"And you expect me to make a choice now, after being in their company for only one evening?"

The king took a deep breath and opened his mouth to speak, but then stopped. He took a step back and gave a small bow. "Forgive me, Queen Nara, if I have offended in any way. It is not my intention. I have been accused of being too brusque and businesslike on occasion. Of course you may take some time to decide, but as I said, I would like this alliance sealed as soon as possible."

Nara cocked her head slightly. "May I ask why you feel there is such urgency?"

The king studied her for a moment before answering. "We have noticed some apparently aggressive actions from an adversary across the sea, and as I have said, there have been disturbing rumors coming from our other borders lately."

"What rumors?"

"There are changes occurring in the Valley of Lhin. Although that is some distance from us, I am concerned that I must do everything I can to ensure the safety of my kingdom. Surely you have heard these rumors as well, since you also share a border with the Lhinians?"

Nara hesitated, wondering how much she should trust this king. She wondered why he would be concerned about Eghan's return to the Valley of Lhin and his marriage. Surely that would mean greater stability, not the opposite. She thought of the premonition she had felt and considered for a moment sharing it with Delmar, but something stopped her.

"I have heard nothing to warrant undue concern," she said, "and rumors are not something I act upon."

The king's eyes narrowed. "Then perhaps you should investigate further."

A chill ran through Nara that almost made her shudder as she studied him, but she nodded. "I will act on that advice."

Delmar nodded back and resumed walking. "Good. In the meantime we would welcome your presence here for as long as you wish. My brothers will be pleased to spend time with you so that you may assess them at your leisure. But I do expect your decision soon, say, by the end of this month?"

"And if I should choose neither of them?"

The king's eyebrows shot up. "That would be most unfortunate indeed, for us both."

In the days that followed the brothers became attentive to Nara's every need. They walked with her, danced with her, rode with her and entertained her with their wit and humor. Talwynn too was almost always by her side, when she was not being courted herself by a string of handsome young men. Nara had come to like the princess and her brothers, but still she did not feel as comfortable with them as she would have liked. Something always niggled in her heart, and often some glance between them set her on edge. And memories of Eghan would not let go.

****

King Delmar was aware of his brother, lurking on the edge of the crowded court. He wished he could banish the misgivings he had about Muirgheal. He knew his brother was ambitious and headstrong but Delmar did not want to believe he was conniving. But he could not ignore the rumors that persisted.

He watched his handsome brother bow to a young woman, lean toward her and whisper in her ear. The girl laughed and cocked her head coyly. Delmar sighed. If only Muirgheal would concern himself with his flirting and leave the politics to him.

A nobleman approached and Delmar was engaged in conversation for some time. When he looked around again Muirgheal was gone. He did not see him again until the evening meal. As they feasted, Delmar wondered if he should confront his brother about what he had heard. He was still considering when Muirgheal leaned toward him and addressed him quietly.

"I would speak with you, brother."

"You are speaking with me, Muirgheal."

"In private."

"Very well. Come." He stood and strode from the room, his brother at his heels. When they entered Delmar's private study he turned on his brother. "What troubles you?"

"The girl is not cooperating."

"She is a queen, Muirgheal, not a girl. And she needs time. She is perhaps overly cautious but she is an intelligent young woman. I am confident she will do what is needed for her country and thereby the same for ours."

"But she shows no sign of making a decision and time is not on our side. We must begin to forge the weapons and ammunition immediately. Belastorian ships could enter our waters any day."

"We have heard only rumors of their intent. We have seen no real signs of aggression."

"And what if we don't? What if all we see is the flash of their cannon? If they come against us in strength now we will not be able to stand against them. We don't have the cannons, or the balls to put in them. We need the Alingan ore, brother. We need it now."

"So what do you propose?" Delmar threw up his hands. "That I lock this queen in my dungeon until she agrees to marry you or your brother?"

When Muirgheal did not answer the king's eyes narrowed. "Muirgheal, what are you scheming?" Delmar noted that his brother's eyes wandered the room.

"Nothing," he said.

"I warn you," the king said. "Do not take this matter into your own hands."

Muirgheal took a deep breath. "We could act, without forming an alliance."

Delmar shook his head. "No."

"The Alingans could not stand against us."

"No!"

Muirgheal opened his mouth to speak again, but sighed and chewed his lip instead.

Delmar moved toward him and put a hand on his arm. "War is never an answer, brother, not even a war we know we would win. Have patience, Muirgheal. Patience."

Muigheal took a step back and bowed stiffly from the waist. "As you wish, Your Majesty." He whirled on his heel and left the room.

Delmar sighed. He knew what his brother had said was true. The Belastorians had long stayed on their side of the sea and even traded with them from time to time but their ships had been seen running close to Brimladin's shores. And they were not cargo ships.

He sank down onto a chair. This was the price of building a prosperous kingdom. Enemies are made only because of their lust to own it. He would talk to Queen Nara again. Perhaps if he shared the urgency with her she would do what must be done immediately.

****

Muirgheal stomped down the long corridor toward the outer courtyard. He was tired of always having to bow to his older brother's wishes, angry that his ideas were once again swept away as foolishness. They were not. The danger to their kingdom was real and if his brother was not willing to act swiftly to ensure their safety then he would have to act alone. The king would undoubtedly thank him later.

Chapter Five

Eghan hefted a heavy pail of water onto the back of their wagon. He had to admit the gypsy medicine Ulhrik forced him to drink morning and night was working. His strength was returning more each day. He had even walked beside the wagon for most of that day as they continued toward the borders of Brimladin. He gripped his right arm. *Except for this,* he thought, *I would be normal again.*

Isham and Latham had gone hunting with some of the men but he wondered where Ulhrik was. It was not like the old man to leave the wagon unguarded. They still did not entirely trust their hosts. Isham and Ulhrik had debated for some time before agreeing to travel with them when they discovered they too were making their way to Brimladin. In the end they decided it would be good cover to disguise themselves as gypsies, and it had worked well. Those they met along the way had paid them no heed.

Eghan glanced down at the rough breeches he now wore. The billowing shirt fit him well and he had to admit it was comfortable. He hoped the disguise would hold. Balor had told them that morning that they were only two days from the city of Brimladin Ula.

Eghan was about to go in search of Ulhrik when he heard a commotion and saw the gypsy leader striding toward him with another man dragging a squirming boy by his arm. Balor's face was flushed, the veins on his neck standing out.

"I ask your forgiveness, my friend," Balor said. He grabbed the boy's arm and dragged him in front of Eghan. "This boy disobeyed my orders and has stolen from you." He held out the leather case that held Eghan's copy of The Book. "He will be given a good thrashing I can assure you," Balor said. He cocked his head. "Or perhaps you would wish to do it yourself. I will demand that his father allow it."

Eghan stared at the satchel, then at the boy, whose eyes were wide with fear. "Leave him be. He can have it," he said, with a wave of his good arm. "I no longer have any use for it."

Balor frowned and opened his mouth to speak but seemed to think again. He nodded at Eghan. "It will not happen again," he said, tucked the satchel under his arm and walked back toward the circle of gypsy wagons.

Eghan saw the other man pull his wide leather belt from around his waist as he dragged the boy with him.

****

Later that day Ulhrik was sitting on the outer edge of the circle of men, close to the cooking fires, when Balor approached him with a worn wineskin in his hand.

"Drink?" the gypsy asked.

Ulhrik took it from his hands and drank, then handed it back with a nod. Balor sank to the ground beside him, lifted it to his lips and gulped. He wiped his mouth with the back of his hand.

"I hope the incident earlier today will not affect our friendship, Ulhrik, nor destroy the trust you have put in me."

"Incident?"

Balor's eyebrows rose. "Your young companion did not tell you?"

Ulhrik waited. Balor took another drink then reached behind him and drew out the leather bag.

Ulhrik could not hide his surprise.

Balor took The Book from its case."One of our young whelps took it from your wagon. Against my orders, you understand, for which he paid with a few strips of his young hide."

The man's hand slid over the soft leather. "I thought I would sell it at the next market we come to, since your young friend said he did not want it back, you understand." He sighed. "It would have fetched a good price in Brimladin Ula." He opened the front cover. "But when I saw this ..."

Ulhrik knew the man was watching his face for a reaction. He stared at the page, the lineage of Eghan's family clear in the branches outlining the descendants of the House of Lhin. He raised his eyes to meet the gypsy's but said nothing.

Balor closed the book, put it back into the bag and handed it to him. "No one else has seen it," he said.

Ulhrik took the book and put out his hand. "Thank you, Balor. This has indeed proved your loyalty to us."

Balor shook hands, then cocked his head. "I will remain loyal, my friend, but I am curious. How is it that a young vagabond is in possession of a book such as this? Did he steal it?" The gypsy's eyes narrowed. "Or is it perhaps his, by right?"

Ulhrik looked into the man's eyes, judging again whether or not to be honest with him.

"The book belongs to him, by birthright," he said.

Balor whistled and his eyes widened. "And can you tell me why the Prince of Lhin is traveling like a gypsy beyond his own kingdom?"

"His kingdom is in ruins. The House of Lhin has fallen, overrun by evil. Eghan is now the Lhinian King but he is without power, and being hunted."

Balor's chin rose. "I had heard rumors. This is news that is good for none of us," he said. He stroked one of his long braids. "Perhaps you should instruct the young king to be more careful that his secret does not become known by those who may not be so concerned with his safety." He nodded to The Book. "Or perhaps you should remove the first pages of this book."

"This book is sacred to me, not because of that

lineage, but because of what lies written on the other pages."

Balor's eyebrows flew up. "Something more important than the written lineage of your king?"

Ulhrik smiled. "Actually, exactly that." He raised the book. "This is the lineage and life of The One True God. It contains His words to us who try to live according to His teachings." Ulhrik looked into the gypsy's eyes. "If I thought you had interest in it I would be pleased to lend it to you, now that I know you can read it."

"That would be a step of trust indeed and I am honored, but, though I do read, it does not come easily to me."

"Then I would be pleased to read it to you."

Balor stared at The Book for some time before nodding his head. "I would be interested."

Ulhrik smiled again. "Shall we meet in the morning, then, before breaking camp?"

Balor nodded again. "At the far end of the pond, away from ..." He hesitated. "Away from the noise of the camp."

He offered the wineskin again. "Shall we drink to seal the agreement?"

Ulhrik drank and handed it back to him. Balor stood and drained the rest. His eyes were dancing when he lifted the skin in salute and walked away.

Ulhrik held the leather bag in his hands for some time before pushing himself up with a sigh. He made his way back to their wagon slowly, his head bowed. The shock of knowing Eghan would so easily let go of something that had once been precious to him weighed heavily upon Ulhrik. *I must do something to bring the boy back. But what? Lord,* he prayed, *what can I do?*

****

Eghan lingered by the gypsies' fires, watching the young women dance. Their skirts flared as they whirled, their jewelry jangling to the rhythm of the music. Eghan found himself caught up in the liveliness of it, their obvious joy stirring him more than he would have admitted. The dance ended and someone called out a name. It quickly became a chant. "Oneida, Oneida."

She stepped forward, her back to him. Something about her long black hair gleaming in the firelight stirred memories of Nara. Eghan pushed them away. Then the girl began to sing, walking slowly around the fire, raising her arms as though she were worshiping. Her voice was pure, sweet, like liquid honey pouring into him. He couldn't understand the words but as he watched her face the song drew a moan from the depths of him that came unexpectedly to his lips. The woman's dark eyes met and locked on his and she took a step toward him but he turned away and ran.

****

Ulhrik was sitting by a small cooking fire, watching Latham settle a kettle on it. Eghan avoided them and climbed into the back of the wagon, intending to sleep. But sleep would not come. He tossed and turned for some time, his arm throbbing and his mind whirling. Each time he closed his eyes he saw Nara's face, her eyes dancing as they had so often when they lived together in Adlair's house. After a while he heard Latham enter the wagon but did not respond when he called his name. Then he felt something poke at his leg and heard Ulhrik's raspy voice telling him to get up and eat.

After some time, he threw off the cover with a growl and strode toward his companions. He took a bowl from Latham and sat near the fire, eating the mixture of fish and vegetables slowly, without speaking. He stayed there as the boy and Isham cleaned up the cooking utensils and laid out their sleeping mats. Eghan jumped when Ulhrik tapped his shoulder with his walking stick.

"Come," he said, and strode away.

Eghan thought to ignore him, but sighed and followed, knowing the old man would not let him rest until he obeyed.

Ulhrik stood with his back to him, staring across the small pond where the gypsies had caught the fish they had just eaten. Eghan steeled himself for the words he suspected would come.

"There is something I want you to do," Ulhrik finally said.

"What?"

The old man turned to face him. "Balor has shown interest in this," Ulhrik held out The Book.

Eghan's heart skipped a beat but he did not reach for it and did not raise his eyes until Ulhrik spoke again.

"I want you to teach him," Ulhrik continued.

Eghan took a step back, shaking his head. "No."

"You will." Ulhrik stepped toward him and grabbed his good arm, forcing The Book into his hand.

"How can I teach what I no longer believe?"

Ulhrik shook his head with that 'oh you young fool' kind of expression that Eghan resented but had so often grudgingly acknowledged was well deserved.

"It is not that you no longer believe, my young Sire, it is that you have allowed self-pity to overshadow your belief and your anger to distort the truth."

Eghan raised his eyes to the old man's. "And do I not have a right to that anger? He has left me with nothing. He torments me with nightmares, or dreams that can never be."

"Oh? So now you attribute the sorrows of this world to Him and have the audacity to say you know the future he has planned?" Ulhrik wrapped his hand around Eghan's and pressed The Book to his chest. "You will meet Balor Engre here tomorrow, before the breaking of the fast and you will teach him. Begin with the gospel of John."

Eghan watched him hobble away. He stared out across the pond for a while, then followed him back to their wagon. The fire was still burning low but Latham and Isham were already asleep, wrapped in their blankets. Ulhrik must have gone to his bed in the wagon. Eghan sat on a stump and laid another log on the fire, then opened the cover of The Book, leaning forward to read by its light. His finger traced the family tree to his mother's name, then his father's and his own. He closed the cover, bitterness burning in him. There would be no further branches to his family's line.

He was about to tuck The Book back into its case when he felt a now familiar nudge. Read. Eghan thought to ignore it, but his fingers lifted the pages of the book. It fell open to Psalm 16. Leaning toward the light, he read. "Keep me safe, my God, for in you I take refuge. I say to the Lord, "You are my Lord; apart from you I have no good thing." I say of the holy people who are in the land, "They are the noble ones in whom is all my delight" (Psalm 16:1-3).

Eghan frowned and closed the book. The holy people who are in the land. What does it mean? he wondered. A soft breeze stirred the trees and Eghan sat up straight as he heard the words, "the ambassadors" breathed into him like a strong current.

The pale light of a crescent moon had risen high before he roused himself from the cold fire and went to his bed.

Chapter Six

Khalwyd woke in darkness. Something was gnawing on his shoulder. He jerked away and the rats scurried out of the cell. He lay on a pile of rank straw but his hands and feet were free. He knew he must have fainted again, but wondered why he was no longer chained. Had he told them about the secret passageways beneath the house of prayer? Had he screamed the words as they flailed the skin from his back? He prayed not, but he could not remember.

He wondered if Eghan and Ulhrik were still there, hidden, perhaps not far from where he now lay. Or had they escaped into the countryside. Where would they go? To the mountains, perhaps, to find Adlair and seek shelter with the Huntsmen. Yes, that would be wise. Damon knew nothing of the alliance Eghan had made with the Huntsmen. Perhaps he did not even know they existed. Once in the mountains, Eghan would be safe.

Khalwyd tried to move, but moaned in pain and lay still again. The putrid smell of the straw and his own blood made him want to retch. Thirst plagued him. When he felt the darkness of unconsciousness start to descend again, he fought against it. The rats would come back. He had to stay awake.

When the cell door creaked he did not have the energy to turn his head. He prayed that the end would come quickly. Then he felt rough hands grab his arms and cried out as he was lifted. It wasn't until he heard a familiar voice that he roused himself and tried to understand what was being said. The voice was loud and angry.

"Get out of my way, or you will take his place when Lord Damon returns."

"But he ..."

"... has ordered that this prisoner be brought to him. And no wonder, with the stench down here. Out of my way!" the voice bellowed again.

Khalwyd moaned as he heard their footsteps come closer. He clenched his jaw in an effort to muffle his own screams as they dragged him out of the cell and up the long stone stairway that led out of the dungeons. It wasn't until they stepped out into the open air that the man who had spoken leaned into him and spoke quietly. "Forgive us for not being more gentle, my friend, but we must appear to be doing Damon's bidding. Take heart. You will be out of his reach soon."

Khalwyd raised his head and looked into Jhonar's eyes. He opened his mouth to speak, but could not. As the men moved forward again, his head jerked back, then fell forward as darkness engulfed him.

When he jerked awake again, Khalwyd's heart thumped in his chest. Then he smelled the sweetness of the hay beneath him and felt something cool and soothing on his back. It was too dark to see anything but he knew from the smell he was no longer in the dungeon. He relaxed back onto the straw, remembering it was Captain Jhonar, once a trusted guard in King Gherin's service, who had carried him away from that nightmarish place. He did not know where he had been taken, but he knew he was safe. He lay in the darkness and thanked God for that deliverance, then slipped back into sleep.

A flickering light woke him again and he tried to sit up. A man's voice stopped him.

"Be still, Khalwyd. You have lost no small amount of blood. Rest is vital."

"Lord Adlair? But how ... I thought you had escaped to the far mountains. Or am I ... where are we?"

"Beneath the house of prayer, my friend, where we will remain until you are strong enough to travel."

"Prince Eghan ... ?"

"Is safely away. We can be assured that The One True God will keep him, and Ulhrik will not allow more harm to come to him."

"Are you sure we are safe here? If we are discovered ..."

The light from a second torch filled the room with its light as Jhonar entered. "We are safe for now, but we should not remain any longer than we must." Jhonar grinned down at him. "Lord Damon is not pleased that you escaped, my friend. I just heard he has put a price on my head and a heftier one on yours, of course."

Khalwyd snorted. "No doubt." He peered up at Adlair. "You both should flee. They have flayed the skin from my back and it will be some time before I am able to move let alone ride. I will follow when I am strong enough."

Adlair laid a hand on his arm. "We will not leave you behind, Khalwyd. Ulhrik's skill was true and these inner reaches are well hid. Besides, Damon will not think to look for you right under his nose. The herbs and salve I have put on your back will heal it quickly. And we have the power of prayer."

Khalwyd sank down on the straw bed and clenched his jaw to keep from moaning. He did not have the strength to argue further. Knowing that Eghan had escaped greatly relieved his mind but he knew he must be diligent in praying for him and for these friends. The days ahead would no doubt prove dangerous for them all.

****

Eghan peered through the trees, his ears perked for the sound of footsteps. He half hoped Balor would not come. Ulhrik could not force him to teach if the gypsy leader did not show interest. The early light cast pale shafts between the trees, their leaves stirring slightly with the breeze. Eghan turned toward the pond and sat down with a sigh. This was a peaceful place, a place like some he had known in the Valley of Lhin. A longing surged up in him for his home but before he had time to acknowledge it a man's voice made him leap to his feet.

"I thought it was Ulhrik who was to meet with me," Balor said.

Eghan started to move away. "I will tell him that is what you prefer."

"No." Balor waved his hand. "You will do. I assume a prince, or should I say a king, reads well?" Eghan's head jerked up.

Balor grinned. "Yes, I know who you are, King Eghan Lhin. Balor gave him a low bow, then straightened and grinned at him. "But as I have told the old man, there is no need to fear. I will not betray you." He walked toward the pond and sat on the trunk of a fallen tree.

Eghan did not move.

"Well?" Balor folded his hands.

Eghan sighed but sat on the ground near him and opened The Book. He read uninterrupted until a noise from the camp caused them both to look toward it.

Balor stood abruptly. "My people are rousing. I must go."

Eghan remained where he was, wondering why the man was so quick to leave. *Perhaps he thinks what I have read to him is all foolishness,* he thought. *And perhaps that will put an end to this.* He could not decide if that pleased him or caused him regret. He sat still for a time, watching a flock of ducks glide over the calm surface of the pond. The stillness seeped into him as a shaft of light flooded over him.

In him was life and that life was the light of all mankind. The light shines in the darkness and the darkness has not overcome it. Eghan closed his eyes and let the words of John 1: 4 & 5 linger in his mind. *But the darkness has overcome it,* he thought. *My father and friends are dead. Damon rules the Valley of Lhin and I am left with nothing.*

"Nothing?"

Eghan's eyes popped open and he leaped up, expecting to see someone standing behind him. But only the ducks stirred, rising from the pond with loud flapping and squawking. The Book had fallen at Eghan's feet. He picked it up, passed his hand over its cover and placed it carefully in its satchel. He glanced around once more, then headed to their wagon. Latham and Isham had already packed up and were harnessing the horse.

Ulhrik came up behind him as he was about to climb in.

"Well?" he asked.

Eghan raised his eyebrows but said nothing.

Ulhrik stared at him, then finally asked again.

"Well? How was the time with Balor?"

Eghan half turned back to the wagon. "I read to him."

"And?"

Eghan sighed. "I read to him and that was all. When the camp began to rouse he ran like a frightened rabbit."

Ulhrik grunted "I will arrange another time tomorrow." He walked away before Eghan could object.

The wagon swayed, its motion and the growing heat making Eghan drowsy as the day wore on. They had decided not to stop at mid-day, eating bread and dried meat as they went. The borders of Brimladin were within reach.

Eghan was asleep when the wagon lurched to a stop and the backboard dropped down as Latham jumped in. As usual, he was excited.

"You'll want to see this, m'lord," he said, pulling on Eghan's sleeve.

Eghan shook him off but climbed out, stretching to rid himself of the drowsiness. He joined Latham and the others as they moved toward the edge of a rugged cliff. What he saw made him stare. A vast valley spread below them, green and vibrant in the sinking light. But it was what was beyond it that made the people gasp and point.

"Brimladin Ula," Isham said. "The finest city and most beautiful castle I have ever seen." He waved his hand to the west of it. "That quarter there is where my wife's family lives. We will seek them out tomorrow."

"Are you sure they will welcome four hungry mouths to feed?" Eghan asked.

Isham shrugged. "My father-in-law is a generous man who makes a good living as a blacksmith. He will welcome us, and help us as he is able, I am sure."

"And the Brimleish?" Ulhrik asked. "Will they welcome a band of gypsies to their doorstep, I wonder?"

Isham's brow furrowed. "Perhaps we should take our leave of this merry band before we arrive?"

Ulhrik shrugged. "We shall see." He glanced at Eghan. "For now we will remain with them." As they turned back to the wagon, he put his hand on Eghan's shoulder. "Balor will meet with you again in the morning, at the edge of the camp, before the breaking of the fast."

Eghan groaned. "Could it not at least be after I have eaten?"

"Balor specified before." He grinned. "Apparently he's an early riser."

"Or prefers a certain amount of secrecy." Eghan glanced sideways at Ulhrik to gauge his reaction.

"Whatever his reasons, we will accommodate him."

They made camp on the bluff that night. Isham pulled their wagon off to the side, away from the rest but Eghan found himself drawn to the gypsies' fires once again. He wandered through their camp and as he listened to the music and watched the women dance he found himself hoping they would remain with these people. Their love of life was infectious and he knew he would miss their exuberance.

He was about to return to their wagon when he heard the woman's voice. It was the same voice that had so moved him before. He followed the sound, turning away from the main fires where the women danced. She was sitting on the back of a wagon, an infant cradled in her arms. She rocked the child as she sang a soft lullaby.

Eghan stayed in the shadows, leaned against a tree and closed his eyes as he listened. The pure love that poured through her voice made tears streak his face as the longing he had tried so hard to push down rose up in him and demanded release. A sob broke from his lips and the woman stopped singing. She stood and stared, then called into the darkness.

Eghan did not understand what she had said, but stepped forward into the light of her fire to relieve her fears. She smiled when she saw him, and the compassion in her eyes made him want to sob again. He stepped back into the darkness. The woman took a step toward him, then stopped."I will pray for you," she said, the English words thick with accent but clear in the night.

Eghan turned and strode quickly back to his wagon.

True to his word, Ulhrik woke him early the next morning. Eghan took The Book and followed him to the edge of the bluff and into a small copse of trees where Balor waited. The gypsy leader sat on the ground and nodded to him to do the same. Eghan sighed but squatted across from him and opened the Book. He resumed reading from the book of John, pausing now and then to look up.

Ulhrik stayed for a time, then moved off in the direction of their wagon. As Eghan read Balor leaned forward, his dark eyes intent on Eghan's face, but he said nothing until Eghan reached the end of the chapter and stopped.

The gypsy leader leaned back against a tree and sighed. "These words intrigue me. Do you believe them?"

Eghan dropped his eyes and shoved the book into its satchel. He held it in his hands for several moments, then finally looked Balor in the eyes. "Yes," he said, the word barely a whisper.

Balor grunted. "Today we will reach the city of Brimladin Ula. Our journey will be at an end, but I do not wish this to end." He waved his hand toward The Book.

Eghan sighed. He realized he too did not want to stop the reading. The story, indeed the very words, had begun to draw him in and to move him once again.

"I will meet with you whenever you wish, to read," he said.

Balor stood. "Good," he smiled and walked away.

When Eghan returned to the wagon he knew Ulhrik watched him intently and Eghan waited for the old man to ask how it had gone. When he did not, Eghan glanced up in time to see a slight smile playing on his lips. Eghan couldn't help but smile as well. *Sly old fox*, he thought, but said nothing to him.

The gypsies made directly for the main square of the town and Eghan marveled at their boldness as they circled their wagons and opened their stalls to trade with the townspeople. Jugglers and acrobats began performing and it seemed every man and child brought out an instrument of some kind to make their music echo through the streets. It wasn't long before they attracted a crowd.

Ulhrik cautioned him to stay hidden while he and Isham went in search of the farmer's relatives, but Eghan's curiosity got the better of him. He pulled his hood over his face, threw a cloak over his wounded arm and wandered among the people, watching as the copper and even some silver coins began to exchange hands. Not all of it was exchanged willingly. Eghan saw more than one boy lift a money pouch from an unsuspecting pocket while men drew their attention with magic tricks and women captivated them with swaying hips and flashing smiles.

The day was almost done before Ulhrik and Isham returned with news that though the farmer's father-in-law had welcomed them warmly he already had guests staying in his home. They would remain with the gypsies for the time being. Eghan did not object.

As the day waned the band folded their stalls back into their wagons and made their way to the edge of the town where they found a good place to camp near a fast flowing creek. As he watched Isham and Latham prepare their meal, Eghan saw Balor approach with a fresh catch of fish. Eghan listened as the two talked and Ulhrik revealed his plan.

"We will seek out honest work," he said.
Balor grinned. "Honest work usually means hard labor, my friend."

Ulhrik nodded. "We are able."

Balor shrugged. "There are other ways."

Eghan had not mentioned the thievery he had witnessed, but it was obvious his guardian was not ignorant of it.

"I am certain there must be need for stonemasons in such a large town," Ulhrik said. "Then we will be able to repay you for your kindness, my friend." He nodded toward the fish Latham was frying on the fire.

"No need," Balor replied with a wave of his hand. He glanced at Eghan. "If the boy will continue with the readings."

Ulhrik waited for Eghan to reply.

He nodded. "I will."

Balor smiled. His gold tooth glinted in the firelight. "Then join us at our campfire tonight." He watched Eghan's face. "Oneida will sing."

Eghan dropped his eyes but looked up again when Balor chuckled.

"Nothing happens in my camp that I do not know about."

Ulhrik cocked his head but said nothing.

Eghan busied himself with chopping some kindling but when Balor walked away Ulhrik did not wait to ask.

"Oneida?"

Eghan shrugged. "She has a beautiful voice."

"Then we will join the gypsies tonight."

After their meal Eghan slipped away before Ulhrik suggested they join the group, wanting to be alone when Oneida sang. As he walked toward the fires he could hear that the music was more raucous than usual. The gypsies were celebrating a good day in the market. He circled the wagons, waiting until there was a good crowd gathered by the fires. He was about to move closer when he heard a horse snort from somewhere in the trees behind him.

He stood still and listened, then heard it again. Curious, he moved toward it, staying in the shadows. It did not take him long to see the soldiers, two of them with the Brimleish emblem clear on their tunics. Two other men who stood with them were a bit younger and clearly not soldiers, by the richness of their clothing. Eghan watched as they secured their horses, pulled their tunics off and exchanged them for those worn by the common people before moving toward the gypsy camp. Eghan thought to report it to Balor, but did not want to bring attention to himself. *No need,* he told himself. *They are no doubt only here to sample what the gypsies freely offer.*

The dancing that night was wild with abandon. But when Oneida stood and moved to the center of the group, the women stopped cavorting and joined the men seated in a large circle. Only one man with a fiddle remained standing. Oneida smiled and nodded to him and he began to play. The sweetness of the sound was outdone only by Oneida's voice, so clear and pure it made goose bumps rise on Eghan's arms. She moved around the circle slowly, smiling as she sang. A small girl left her mother's side and took Oneida's hand as she walked. The woman smiled down at her but did not stop singing.

When she reached the place where Eghan's friends sat, she hesitated, her eyes searching their faces. Eghan made sure he was well hidden. Then she moved on. He was surprised when she stopped, turned and looked directly toward him. He took a step back, deeper into the darkness, but she did not move. He couldn't be sure but it seemed the intensity of her song increased, and she remained there until her song was done. By that time Eghan could hardly breathe and once again the longing in him threatened to spill out. He desperately tried to keep that from happening. All eyes peered into the darkness that he hoped still hid him.

Two other fiddlers suddenly leaped up and struck a fast tune, the other man joining them as the women clapped their hands and pulled their partners up to dance around the fires once again.

Eghan was thankful that the spell had been broken. He wasn't sure how much longer he could have contained his emotions. Oneida still stared into the trees where he stood.

Ulhrik stepped forward, took her arm and spoke quietly with her as they walked away. Eghan strained to hear what they were saying but the music was too loud. He turned to leave, moving quickly away from the center of the group. He made his way back to his own wagon and went directly to his bed. Perhaps tomorrow he would ask Oneida the meaning in the words she sang. Perhaps she could tell him why it stirred such strong emotions in him.

The next day Eghan was shaken awake and told to get up. He opened his eyes to see Ulhrik staring down at him. He rolled away but the old man's stick poked at him.

"Balor will be waiting," he said.

Eghan groaned but threw off the cover, pulled The Book from its hiding place and lowered himself down from the backboard.

The old man pointed with his stick and Eghan walked into the woods. He found Balor near the creek, standing beside a woman squatting over a small cooking fire, a pot of porridge burbling on it.

"I thought I might as well eat while you read," he said. The woman straightened, poured the porridge into a wooden bowl and turned to hand it to him.

Eghan caught his breath as Oneida lifted her eyes to his. She smiled but said nothing. He gulped a deep breath, sat on a nearby log and busied himself with pulling The Book from its case. He looked up when Balor stood over him, holding a bowl out to him.

"And I thought perhaps you would be hungry as well."

Eghan nodded and took the bowl.

Balor's grin was wide as he waved his hand at the young woman. "I believe you have met my daughter?"

The jerk of Eghan's head was involuntary and Balor's grin turned to almost a smirk. The man waved at the bowl in Eghan's hand.

"She is a good cook. Another of her many talents."

Eghan nodded but did not dare look at her. They ate in silence. When he was done Balor stretched out with his back to a tree. Eghan was aware of Oneida as she walked to the river to wash out the cooking pot. He was also very much aware when she returned, stood behind her father and waited. Eghan spooned the last of the porridge into his mouth and picked up The Book.

He had marked the place where they had stopped and was about to begin when Balor said, "Read me that last bit again."

Eghan cocked his head. "The trial?"

"Yes. Read that again."

He turned back to the beginning of chapter eighteen and read. He expected that Balor would ask a question or make a comment but he did not.

And once again, when they heard the gypsies begin to move about in their camp, Balor told him to stop reading. He nodded his thanks, spoke briefly to Oneida and quickly walked away. The girl gathered her cooking utensils and started to follow her father.

Eghan leaped to his feet. "What was that song about? The one you sang last night."

She smiled. "It was a song about broken hearts and our longing for true love. It was a song, too, about finding the true source of love." She cocked her head at him. "I know you have found that source, as I have, yet you still carry a great weight of sorrow."

"That source," Eghan replied, "you speak of the One True God?"

She nodded. "I do."

"How is it you know Him but the rest of your people do not?"

"My mother, she was not one of us. And she was a believer. Before she died she shared her joy with me but my father was in too much pain to accept. When he learned that I had, he was so enraged that he burned my mother's copy of The Book. I have prayed for several years that God would restore it to me and draw my people to Himself." She stared at The Book in Eghan's hand. "You are the answer to that prayer."

Eghan shook his head. "All I have done is read."

"And surely you know that is enough."

"Your father never comments, never asks a question."

"Yet he invited me here today, so I too could listen."

Eghan looked down at The Book. "Perhaps it is you who should read it. I am no longer worthy of it."

When she did not reply he looked up. Once again the compassion in her eyes almost undid him.

"And perhaps it is your pain that will open my father's ears, open his heart."

She smiled again and walked away.

Chapter Seven

"My lord, good news." The captain burst into the great hall, dragging a young boy who struggled in his grasp.
Damon strode toward him. "What?"
"This gypsy brat has seen the prince. I heard him talking about it in the market."
Damon grabbed the front of the boy's shirt and almost lifted him off his feet. "Where?" he bellowed.
The boy squirmed. "Let me go and I'll tell you."
Damon shook him. "You will tell me now you little mongrel, or I will whip it out of you."
The boy's eyes went wide. "He's with my uncle's band. My father and I traveled with them for a time."
"Are you sure it was Prince Eghan Lhin?"
The boy nodded. "I think so. Their wagon joined my uncle's band just before we arrived. He gave them clothes to wear but they're no gypsies, that is plain."
Damon's chin went up. "Their wagon? Who travels with him?"
"An old man and a big farmer, and a boy about my age. I knew it was the prince when I heard he

has a gimp arm and I ... I saw his book. I overheard them talkin' about what was in it. They said it was the lineage of the House of Lhin." My father gave me a thrashin' for takin' it from their wagon.

Damon smiled. "And where is your uncle's band, boy? Be clear."

"I dddon't know, exactly."

Damon struck him across the face with the back of his hand. The boy cried out and reeled back. He would have fallen to the floor had Damon not had hold of him.

"Where?" Damon bellowed again.

"Th...they wander ... I ... I don't know exactly where they were goin'."

"Where were they when you last saw them?" Damon shook him and raised his hand again. "Tell me!"

"In the woods," the boy said, cringing. "In the woods, in the far reaches of the valley, only a few day's journey from the border."

Damon let go of his shirt and turned to the soldier. "Take a troop and leave immediately." He smirked at the boy. "This brave young lad will lead you." He gripped the boy's shoulder until he winced. "Won't you my young friend?"

The boy swallowed hard and nodded as tears seeped from his eyes.

"Be sure no harm comes to the prince," Damon ordered the captain, "but kill the others and anyone else who gets in your way. There will be a pouch full of gold for the man who brings me the prince."

The soldier smiled and nodded. "Yes, my lord. We'll get 'im, sir."

Damon's eyes narrowed. "You had better."

The captain checked the rope that tied the boy's hands to the saddle. He peered into his face. "Take us there directly, boy, you understand? Try to trick me and you'll regret it."

The boy nodded. The captain gave the order to mount up and they trotted out of the castle's grounds and along the straight road that led out of the Valley of Lhin. As they reached the woods the captain glanced over his shoulder. Some of the men looked half asleep. The captain cursed under his breath. He had no way of knowing which of these men were truly loyal to Lord Damon. So many had deserted recently, some from this very troop. Truth be told, the Captain didn't blame them. Damon was not known for his consideration, even to the men in his own army.

"Wake up," he bellowed. "Keep your eyes open. We're looking for a band of gypsies. They are sly and sneaky. If you see anything, hear anything, sing out." He did not tell the men who they were looking for but he knew most of them would have guessed by now. He hoped they would all follow orders when the time came. He wanted that pouch of gold. He tugged on the rope attached to the boy's horse and nudged his horse into a canter.

"There." The boy pointed with his chin. "By the pond. That's where they were last time I saw him."

The captain cursed. There were no wagons, no sign of life in the small meadow below them. He kicked his horse and they trotted toward the spot.

The remains of small fire pits could be seen as they approached. One of the soldiers dismounted and put his hand over one of them. He looked up at the captain and shook his head.

"They're long gone," he said.

"Look for tracks," the captain bellowed. I want to know which way they went."

The men wandered around the area until one of them gave a shout. "Here, captain. They've headed north."

"Mount up!"

They followed the tracks for a short distance but rain and weather had erased anything further. They continued heading north but saw no sign of a gypsy camp. The captain had rarely been beyond these borders. The country they were heading into was a mystery to him. When they stopped for the night he tied the boy securely to a tree. Then he prepared a plate of food and squatted in front of him.

"Where would they go?" he asked, lifting a spoon full of beans into his own mouth.

The boy's eyes were riveted on the spoon but he shook his head. "I don't know."

"Too bad," the captain said and licked his lips. "These beans are quite good." He picked up a cup and slurped the water, then tossed the remainder on the ground. "You must be thirsty too, aren't ye?"

The boy nodded.

"Then tell me, where would they go?"

Tears seeped out of the boy's eyes. "Brimladen," he said quietly.

The captain smiled. "How far?"

"I don't know. I've never been there before."

"How far do you think?"

The boy shrugged. "A week, maybe two."

The captain patted the boy's cheek. "Good boy." He stood and walked away.

****

"We will seek work today," Ulhrik said. "The gypsies are going to return to the square in the town. We will go with them, then slip away and see what we can find."

Eghan said nothing. He rubbed his lame arm. Who will hire a maimed workman? he wondered. He hoped against hope there was someone who would. He was eager to find something to do besides wander the land.

It did not take the gypsies long to set up their stalls and begin their performances to lure the people to them. Eghan was watching a man juggle three swords when he became aware of a buzz among the small group that had gathered. He turned just as the crowd parted and a line of soldiers approached. The sword juggler stopped immediately and slipped away. The soldiers moved on to the nearest stall where two old women were selling lace.

"Where is your leader?" One of the soldiers demanded.

The old women shook their heads and replied in their own language, shrugging their shoulders and frowning. The soldiers moved on to the next stall, and the next, meeting with the same response. Eghan couldn't help but grin at their frustration but his grin faded when one of the soldiers suddenly pointed.

"There," he cried out. "She's the one."

The troop turned as one and quickly captured their prey. Oneida screamed when two of them grasped her arms. Balor was quick to appear.

"I am the leader of this clever band," he said, his gold tooth glinting as he smiled. "Surely this young maiden has done nothing to offend."

Eghan saw the anger gleam in his eyes and was relieved when, at the captain's signal, the soldiers let go of Oneida's arms.

"We wish her no harm, sir," the captain said. "But it has come to the attention of our king that this young woman's voice could charm the birds from the trees."

Eghan remembered the two soldiers and the other two young men he had seen at the gypsy's camp.

Balor gave a short laugh. "True, true." His eyes narrowed. "And such talent is worth its weight in gold, is it not?"

The soldier smirked. "No doubt she will be well paid if she is willing to perform in the king's court."

Oneida gasped and shook her head at her father but Balor ignored her.

"I'm sure it would be her delight, my friend. And there are others whose talents would greatly entertain the king and his lords and ladies. Perhaps we should bring more than just a song?"

The soldier glanced around and nodded. "After the noon meal then. Come to the castle gates." His voice turned stern. "But if there is any funny business from any of you ..."

Balor's eyebrows shot up. "We would never dream of it, sir. Never dream of it."

The soldier grunted. "Don't bring your whole band. A few jugglers and musicians will suffice."

Balor gave him an exaggerated bow. The soldiers marched away.

Oneida took a step toward her father, shaking her head again. "I do not wish to do this, father. Please, don't make me go there."

Balor put a hand on her shoulder. "There is no need to fear, my girl. You are a prize to them." He touched her cheek. "And I will be with you." He looked over her shoulder and stared at Eghan, then leaned toward her and said softly, "And perhaps we can convince another prince to attend us."

Oneida whirled and stared at Eghan. Balor clapped his hands and told the gypsies to resume their dealings. As the crowd quickly dispersed Balor approached Eghan, his smile now more sincere.

"Would you accompany us? Your presence would secure Oneida's safety."

"Why should it?" Eghan asked. "To all I am just another gypsy."

"But surely there is no need to disguise yourself in the court of King Delmar? I will even give your clothes back to you. The boots I have already sold, sadly."

Ulhrik stepped forward. "We cannot risk revealing his identity, Balor. There may be spies in this court."

Balor frowned. "Very well, accompany us as gypsies then."

Ulhrik nodded. "That we can do."

Balor's smile grew. "Gypsies invited to court. I am looking forward to this."

Eghan glanced around him as they stood at the high iron gates of the castle of Brimladin Ula. What a rag-tag bunch we are, he thought. Gypsy jugglers and musicians, an old prophet and a maimed king in disguise, all about to enter a royal court. *Is this part of your plan, Lord? Or do you even have one for me anymore?*

A guard appeared and the gates swung open. Three carriages rolled to a stop and they were invited to ride. Oneida leaned out the window as the carriage whisked them across a cobble-stoned bridge and came to a stop in front of the formidable doors of the castle.

As Eghan stepped down he looked up at the gleaming white stone of the fortress. He noticed Ulhrik did the same. The structure was impressive. Eghan knew Ulhrik's keen eye took in every inch of the stone. They were ushered into the castle and marched down a long gleaming corridor. Even Eghan was in awe. This was far more grand than his father's house.

They came to a stop in front of another set of high wooden doors. Eghan's mind flew back to the day he had returned to his father's court, remembering the joy he had felt that day when his father embraced him. The deep longing for home surged through him again and he almost groaned. He thought to try and slip away. He had no desire to see more of the opulence of this realm. But before he could think how to do it, the doors swung open and he heard a page announce them. He tugged his hood further over his face and followed the others into the great hall.

People parted as the band was led toward the dais at the far end of the room. Balor stepped forward and bowed before the king and the two younger men standing at his side. Eghan moved to a place where he could see their faces more clearly. Were these the two men he had seen disguising themselves at the gypsy's camp?

"We are honored to be here, Your Majesty," Balor said.

King Delmar's eyes swept across the group. He waved his hand toward Muirgheal and Brimwell. "It is my brothers who have asked you here. I trust your performance will no doubt stand up to their praise?"

"I assure you it will, Sire."

The king waved his hand again. "Get on with it then."

Balor turned and clapped his hands. The musicians immediately struck up a tune and the young women began to dance as the jugglers moved among them, their balls and swords whirling into the air. A man with a small dog began giving it signals to perform its tricks.

Eghan and Ulhrik stepped back into the crowd. Eghan hoped they would not be conspicuous by their lack of performance. He was thinking of trying to make his exit when he heard a young woman's voice behind him.

"Oh Nara, look at that silly dog!"

Eghan turned and found himself staring into the deep dark eyes belonging to the one he knew so well.

Nara's heart almost stopped when she saw who stood before her. She almost threw herself into his arms but then remembered where she was and the many eyes that were watching. Before she could move or say a word Talwynn grabbed her hand and pulled her away. Nara wrenched her hand free and turned back but Eghan was gone. She whirled around, searching the crowd but could not see any sign of him. Had she really seen him? Or was it her imagination? Why would he be here? Why would he be dressed like a gypsy? Why would he hide from her? The questions swirled in her mind until she groaned out loud.

"Queen Nara? What is it?" Muirgheal peered at her intently.

Nara shook her head. "Nothing, Prince Muirgheal. I just thought I saw someone I knew. But I am sure I must have been mistaken."

Muirgheal took her hand and placed it on his arm. "Then come, enjoy this raucous band. They will take your mind off your worries and I assure you, the best is yet to be seen."

Nara allowed him to escort her to the outer edge of the circle of gypsies. She tried to focus on the entertainers but could not help peering around the room from time to time. The thought that Eghan was here, had been within arm's reach, made her stomach churn and her pulse race. But it wasn't until the gypsies suddenly stopped their antics and a young woman stepped forward and began to sing that Nara felt her heart would break in two.

The girl's voice trembled a bit at first, but then she seemed to gain confidence as she closed her eyes and let the song pour out. Nara was completely captivated and it wasn't until the sound ceased that she realized she had been weeping. She brushed the tears away quickly with her free hand as Muirgheal patted the one draped across his arm.

"Very moving, was it not?" he said, his eyes on Oneida as the audience erupted in applause. "The angels of heaven could not sing more sweetly."

Nara nodded but dared not speak. Muirgheal was suddenly attentive, his eyes showing his concern.

She pulled her hand out of the crook of his arm.

"I'm sorry, Prince Muirgheal. I am afraid I'm not feeling well. Please excuse me." She turned on her heel and fled.

****

Eghan had stayed a safe distance from her but could not bring himself to leave. He moved among the crowd, always careful to keep out of Nara's view, but his eyes never left her face. Why was she here? She should have been at home. Did she not know what had happened in the Valley of Lhin? He almost groaned out loud when she turned and smiled at the young man who propelled her on his arm. Eghan recognized him as one of the men he had seen with the soldiers in the gypsy's camp. His heart sank as the realization hit him. One of the king's brothers. Of course. She was being courted. A lovely young queen with a newly-established kingdom would be ripe pickings. An alliance would be to the benefit of both kingdoms. Someone jostled him and he turned away. Then Oneida began to sing.

Eghan tried to flee but the crowd pressed around him and he was disoriented. Where were the doors? He had to get out. He could not bear to hear this song again, not here, not now. At last he was able to force his way through and found the doors. He stumbled through them and down the corridor until he could no longer hear Oneida's voice. Then he pressed his back to a wall and sank down. He pulled his hood over his face, ignoring the footsteps that went past him as he pulled his knees up and wrapped his one good arm around them. It was all he could do to keep from sobbing.

It was Ulhrik who found him there as the gypsies began to take their leave. The old man said nothing to him, only took his arm, pulled him to his feet and turned him toward the outer court. Eghan was glad to leave the place but longed to stay, longed to look just once more into those eyes, longed to hear her voice. *God,* he thought, *why are you torturing me?*

****

Nara raised her head when her handmaid entered the chamber and began chattering on about how wonderful the gypsies were.

Brynna stopped, her mouth open, and stared. She was on her knees at her mistress's side instantly. “My lady, what is it? What has upset you?"

Nara drew in a deep breath and shook her head. "It is only foolishness, Brynna. I am fine now."

"But why were you crying?"

Nara stood and walked to the window seat. "I thought ... I thought I saw Prince Eghan, in the great hall."

"Prince Eghan? But surely he would have been announced."

"He was dressed like a gypsy."

"A gypsy? Then surely it was not him but another who only resembles him."

"Yes, of course, that must be the case. But seeing him, or someone like him, just for the briefest of moments, and then listening to that young girl sing ..." She sighed again and sat down on the window seat. "I'm afraid it has undone me."

Brynna patted her hand. "Shall I make you a cup of tea, my lady? And find some sweetbreads for you?"

Nara smiled at the girl and nodded. "That would be lovely, Brynna. Thank you."

The girl jumped up and left the chamber, then popped her head back in. "Oh, I almost forgot. The princes have asked you to join them in the morning, in the courtyard." She giggled. "It seems they have arranged a performance of their own for you."

The morning dawned bright and clear and as the sunshine beamed into her room, Nara relaxed. She felt as though the shadows of the day before had passed, like the faint wisps of a bad dream. She could not have seen Eghan in the great hall. And even if she had, it did not change her situation. The king had pressed her again to make a decision and she knew she must do so before leaving for home, which should be soon. She felt she had already stayed too long. She sighed as she pushed back the heavy covers and looked around for her plain dress.

She did like the brothers; both of them seemed to have gentle and kind spirits and they certainly were entertaining. But something held her back. Something kept her from completely letting her guard down when she was with them. Muirgheal especially gave her pause. And the thought of marrying one of them, or anyone else, left her with a deep coldness that she could not shake.

She wondered if King Delmar would hold a grudge against her and her people if she refused both of his brothers. Would he still be willing to form an alliance without demanding a marriage? Or would he turn against them, perhaps even come against them in force? She sighed again. Gage was right. They could not afford another enemy on their borders.

She was about to call for Brynna when the door opened and the girl rushed in. "It's the princess Talwynn, my lady. She wishes to see you and she has a gift." Brynna's eyes danced.

"Then help me dress quickly, Brynna."

"No, my lady. Don't dress yet. Just pull your robe about you."

Nara frowned. "I can't greet the princess in my night dress, Brynna."

Brynna giggled. "Yes you can. Trust me." She helped Nara pull the robe on and raced back to the door.

Talwynn stepped in, a flowing green gown in her hands and two maidservants following with other clothing in their arms. "I hope you are not offended,

Queen Nara," the princess said quickly, "but ... well, I thought perhaps you would like these. I have too many dresses in my closets now and I would be so delighted if you would accept these as my gifts to you, as a friend." She searched Nara's face.

Fighting back tears, Nara nodded. "Thank you, thank you." Was all she could manage.

Talwynn waved her hand and the servants spread the clothing across the bed. "There's a riding habit too." Talwynn grinned. "My brothers enjoy riding, and hunting of course."

Nara embraced her and thanked her again as she left the room. As Brynna chose a dress for her to wear she thought perhaps her assessment of this family was too harsh. Perhaps it would be best if she agreed to join her lineage to theirs. She wondered what the mischievous brothers had in store for her this morning. She finished her breakfast quickly, smoothed out the folds in her new frock and went in search of them.

As Nara approached the cobbled courtyard she could hear the whack of wood on wood and now and then a shout which she knew was from the mouth of either Muirgheal or Brimwell. She pushed open the door and stepped outside just as Muirgheal bested his brother and stood over him, the point of his wooden sword pushing into his younger brother's chest. Both jumped up when they saw her.

"Queen Nara, what a delight to see you." Muirgheal bowed. "You are looking lovely this morning." Nara thought she detected a slight smirk in his voice. Did he recognize the dress as one belonging to his sister? Before she could consider it more his voice changed and seemed eager and concerned.

"I trust you slept well and are feeling better today?"

Nara almost squirmed under the intense look in his eyes and the flattery on his lips. "Yes," she answered. "I am feeling quite well now, thank you."

"Good." Muirgheal saluted her with his sword and circled his brother. "Because we have decided on a duel to the death. Today you must choose which one of us you will marry."

Brimwell turned with his brother and whacked him on the backside with his wooden sword, then danced away. "And I am quite certain it will be me, after this display of my excellent swordsmanship."

"Ha!" Muirgheal said, whirling to face him. He brandished his sword in the air. "We shall see." He put one hand behind his back and advanced on Brimwell as though he were fencing. "En guarde, brother."

Nara laughed as the two princes pranced around each other, wooden swords held at ridiculous angles, their faces contorted into mock ferociousness.

"What?" Brimwell stood erect and faced her. "You find this amusing, Queen Nara?" His voice teased and his eyes danced. "Do you not believe we will fight to the death? Only one of us can win your hand."

Muirgheal tossed his sword in the air, skipped around Brimwell, caught the hilt and brought the broad side of it down on his brother's backside with a loud whack. Brimwell leaped away with a shout, made his face into a comical frown and charged back. Muirgheal stepped aside at the last moment and whacked him again. Brimwell clutched his backside and high-stepped away.

Nara's hand flew to her mouth but it was only to try and disguise her laughter. Brimwell was suddenly on his knees at her feet. "Please, my lady, pick me. My brother may be somewhat better with a sword but I have a quicker wit, I assure you. I will continually keep you entertained."

Muirgheal skidded to a stop beside his brother. "But you must know I am the more intelligent brother, and more worthy of your hand."

Nara shook her head and laughed. "You both have kept me well entertained for the past several weeks and for that I am grateful. It has been a welcome diversion from the stresses of running my country. But I must return there soon."

"Of course," Brimwell clapped his hands. "To prepare for the wedding!"

"And what if I choose neither of you?"

The two young men looked at one another with mock incredulity. "She wouldn't," Brimwell said.

"She can't," Muirgheal responded.

Nara thought she caught a glint of something other than humor in his eyes but chose to ignore it. "Oh yes, she can," she said and turned away. "And she very well may."

The brothers scrambled to their feet and ran after her. "Please, my lady," they both chimed. "Don't leave us here to a fate worse than death," Brimwell blocked her way. "Take us to your realm of ore and ... " He turned to his brother. "What else do they have there?"

Muirgheal put a finger to his chin and frowned as though deep in thought. Then he raised it into the air and shouted, "Fine venison!"

Nara laughed out loud and shook her head again. "I cannot imagine why you would not wish to remain in your own realm. A fate worse than death? Surely not."

Brimwell's head bobbed. "Living with our humorless brother is more than we can bear, my lady."

"And what about me?"

They whirled around to see Talwynn standing in the doorway, her hands on her hips."Will you abandon me to stay here alone with our humorless brother?"

The two young men ran to her side. "You already have more suitors than you can stand, Talwynn," Brimwell said. "And you've just been announced. You'll be married off soon and then it will be one of us that will be left alone." He grinned at Nara. "Unless the Queen is gracious and will acquiesce to take us both to her court in Alinga Territory."

Nara smiled. "You may visit my kingdom and my court, when I have one, at any time you wish. Of course I would open my home to you all." Her smile widened as their faces beamed. "But marriage is another, and a much more serious matter."

Muirgheal hid his wooden sword behind his back and nodded. "So it is, my lady. We do not mean to make less of it by our foolery. It is a serious matter indeed, with serious consequences."

Something in the look he gave her made Nara shiver. When he stepped to her side and offered his arm everything in her suddenly screamed, "run!" When he took her hand and laid it on his arm she almost pulled away. Then his voice softened.

"We both understand it is a serious matter, made all the more so by the recent news."

"Recent news?"

Talwynn put her hand on Muirgheal's arm as he opened his mouth to speak. "That is why I have come in search of you, Nara. My brother the king wishes to speak with you immediately. There is news you must hear and I am afraid it is not good."

Nara pulled away from Muirgheal and followed Talwynn through the tall doors, the two brothers following behind.

The king was in a small study near his chamber. He turned as Talwynn opened the door without knocking and ushered Nara inside. The brothers stood outside the door until Delmar waved his hand to invite them in.

"It is best you are all here," the king said, then stepped forward and took Nara's hand, leading her to a chair by the window. He sat opposite and leaned forward as he spoke.

"I am afraid there is bad news, Queen Nara, news that I am sure will affect us all in the days to come. A messenger has come from your homeland. The rumors we spoke of earlier have been confirmed. The house of Lhin has fallen."

Nara leaped up. "What? But how could that have happened?"

"By treachery, I understand. The valley has been overrun by an army led by a man calling himself Lord Damon Gille. The Lhinian king is dead."

Nara opened her mouth but at first no words would come out. She sat down again and tried to gain control. "And his son?" she asked. "Prince Eghan? What of him?"

The king shook his head "There is no news of the prince but he is presumed to also be dead."

"Eghan." It was barely a whisper. She leaped up again. "I must leave at once."

King Delmar put a hand on her arm. "Your carriage is being prepared for the morning as we speak. I will send a full escort with you." He turned to Muirgheal. "You will go as well, brother."

Muirgheal nodded and turned to the door.

Nara shook her head. "I thank you, but that is not

necessary, King Delmar. I have my own escort."

"I must insist, Queen Nara. Your escort is small. If anything were to happen to you on your way, I would feel responsible. Please, allow my brother and my knights to join your own and keep you safe until you reach your homeland."

Nara gave a quick curtsy. "Very well, and thank you again. I wish to leave as soon as possible."

The king nodded. "I would hope you might make a decision about our alliance before leaving?"

Nara's head flew up. "I do favor an alliance, King Delmar, but I cannot and will not make a decision that is tied to my personal future and the future of my people, under these circumstances. I hope you will have patience with me."

The king stood straight and bowed. "Very well. I understand. And I wish you a safe journey."

Chapter Eight

The captain did not want to admit it, but there was a good possibility they were lost. They had seen no further sign of the gypsy caravan nor any sign that they were getting close to this place called Brimladin Ula. All they saw was thick bush that seemed to get thicker and darker as they went. At times it was difficult to find any kind of pathway through and those they did find turned into game trails that led in circles. The captain knew his men were not happy. These woods were too dark, the country too unfamiliar. He could hear them whispering and grumbling behind him.

He was about to call a halt to rest when he thought he saw a flash of something red moving off to his left. He raised his hand and the troop came to a quick halt. The men all peered around them, their hands instinctively going to their weapons, but they neither saw nor heard anything. The woods were silent. *Too silent*, the captain thought. He nudged his horse on, looping the lead rope around his wrist a second time as he jerked the boy's horse forward.

He dared not blink as he peered into the trees, his heart racing as he looked back at his men. They were all staring into the woods, swords drawn. In that instant a man leaped out of the trees and grasped the lead rope, tugging the captain to the ground. He heard his wrist snap as the rope was whipped away. Before he could gain his feet the boy and his horse had disappeared into the thick bush.

The captain gave the order to pursue. The soldiers crashed through the thick bushes, cursing at the brambles and thorns that caught at their clothing and ripped at their faces. They found no trace of the horse or the boy. It was as though the forest had swallowed them up. The captain did find a wide red sash tied to a tree branch. No doubt a message left to taunt him.

"Keep looking!" the captain screamed but it did not take long for them to realize they were going in circles. As night began to fall he finally called a halt to the search and ordered them to make camp. The pain in his wrist kept him awake through the night.

When the morning came he could not ignore the fact that he now had several less men and horses than he'd had when they had set out. As they ate their meager breakfast he noticed the men staring at him. He knew what they were thinking. To return without their prey was unthinkable. Lord Damon would not hesitate to execute the lot of them, as an example if not simply out of rage.

The captain stood up and looked around at the men. Then he reached up to the lapel of his uniform, ripped the insignia from it and threw it into the fire. One by one the men did the same. It did not take them long to distribute the provisions that were left among themselves and disperse into the woods. The captain was left alone, standing by the cold fire pit, cradling his hand.

****

Damon paced in the great hall that had once belonged to the Lhinian king. His adviser stayed at his heels.

The news of the desertion of the troop that had gone in search of the gypsy camp had put him into a rage but now he had another problem, and an equally vexing one.

"Khalwyd of Stohl must be found and executed." Damon spun on his heel, almost running into the man behind him. "Rumors of his escape are spreading and that is feeding a climate of rebellion." He leaned on a table strewn with papers. "It must not be allowed to take root."

Two soldiers entered but remained by the doors. He turned on them. "Well?"

One of the men stepped forward. "They have vanished, my lord. We have searched the town and the countryside but can find no trace of the captain or the prisoner."

Damon cursed and pounded the top of the table, making the men jump. "Someone must know something. Drag anyone who shows any sign of defiance into the streets and flog them until they give us the information we want. I have heard rumors of prayer meetings and gatherings where they are worshiping their god. Find out where they are being held, disperse them and punish those responsible. Show no mercy. Do you hear me?"

"Yes, my lord." They stomped from the room.

Damon moved to a window and looked out. The market place was almost deserted.

His adviser stepped to his side. "The new taxes and confiscation of food is taking its toll. The farmers are hoarding their produce, hiding it from us."

Damon turned on him. "Then see that they are punished! We will need more food and funds as the army increases in size. Hungry men aren't inclined to be loyal."

The adviser bowed, mumbled his agreement and took his leave.

Damon steadied his breathing. This entire kingdom had grown soft under Gherin Lhin's leadership. No doubt there would be much moaning and complaining until the people became accustomed to a new and better way. He smiled to himself and looked at the far away horizon. A way that would make him rich and powerful, especially once they invaded Alinga Territory and took control of the mines. Then they could turn their attentions elsewhere, to even more lucrative endeavors. Damon smirked. He didn't need the prince. He would rule this kingdom and eventually the territories around it with a rod of iron.

****

Jhonar squeezed himself between two buildings and waited for the column of soldiers to pass by. It was getting harder to make his way among the people without coming upon Damon's men and each time he ventured out he held his breath. If he were recognized and betrayed ... he didn't want to think about what Damon would do to him to extract any information about Khalwyd and their young king. He had relied on the fact that most of the people bore no love for their new leader nor his men, but today he had heard a rumor that the bounty on his head, and Khalwyd's head, had been doubled. Many were going hungry because most of their food and silver was being taken from them. Jhonar feared someone eager to feed his children might be tempted to turn him over to Damon's men for a sack of coin.

He clutched the satchel of bread and vegetables he had just bought and waited until he could no longer hear the soldiers' boots pounding the earth. Then he stepped into the street, tugged his hood far over his face and took a circuitous route back to the entrance to the tunnel that led beneath the house of prayer. As he rounded the final corner he heard a woman scream. Jhonar stepped into a dark entryway and listened.

The door opposite burst open and a man was

flung into the street. Two soldiers were upon him instantly, beating and kicking him while a third held a hysterical woman by her arms. Another soldier emerged from the house and threw a book into the mud beside the bleeding man. "You will both pay for your disobedience," the soldier growled. "Take them away."

Jhonar pressed back against the wall as they were dragged off. His heart stopped when the captain peered about, then stared directly at him. Jhonar prayed for the darkness to hide him. When the man finally moved off Jhonar almost collapsed with relief. He waited for what seemed like hours to make sure no one was near when he entered the entrance to the tunnel. Adlair met him half way to their hiding place, a lit torch in his hand."I feared something had happened, Jhonar. You took too long."

"I had to take extra precautions, my lord. Damon's men are everywhere. They are arresting anyone caught with a copy of The Book. And the price on Khalwyd's head has been raised. I fear it may become too dangerous for any of us to buy food in the marketplace now. We must find another way.

Adlair gave a quick nod. "Or leave sooner than we had planned."

"But is he able?"

"I had hoped to wait a while longer, but staying is putting us all in danger of being caught. And we cannot allow that to happen." He tapped Jhonar's arm. "Come, captain, we will discuss it with the others."

The discussion was brief. They agreed to leave the next night.

It had fallen to Jhonar to secure horses for their journey but he returned with none. "They've confiscated almost every horse in the town," he explained. "Even if I could find one or two, we would attract too much attention if we attempted to leave with them."

"Just as well," Khalwyd said. "I don't think I could ride but I might be able to manage to walk."

"Then we must go on foot. Once we get beyond the woods on the north side of the town we may be able to buy a wagon from a farmer." Jhonar reached into a sack. "But in the meantime, these will fortify us for the journey."

Khalwyd smiled at the two cooked birds that dangled from the captain's hand. "A feast indeed," he said. "Well done, captain."

They ate mostly in silence until Adlair leaned forward and put a hand on Jhonar's arm. "What is it, my friend? You seem to be musing over something."

Jhonar hesitated, glanced at Khalwyd and spoke. "You know my loyalty is to the House of Lhin, Lord Adlair. If I leave now I will feel as though I will be running away and betraying that trust. Today I overheard some men in the street talking about rumors of pockets of resistance to Damon's rule. I feel my time would be better spent aligning myself with them and fighting for the restoration of our king, from within the kingdom."

Khalwyd pulled the last of the meat from a bone and nodded. "I agree. My goal is to find Eghan and bring him back to reclaim the throne that belongs to him. Knowing there are brave men loyal to him here would make that goal that much more attainable, especially if those men are ready to fight when needed."

"If there are men loyal to the house of Lhin mustering a resistance they will need a leader." Jhonar looked at Adlair. "I will go with you to the other side of the woods," he said, "then I will return and search them out."

Adlair sighed. "And we will pray for you and all those brave enough to join you."

Chapter Nine

The driver was told not to spare the horses and he took that advice to heart. Their carriage rattled and shook as it tore over the rough road toward Alinga Territory. Nara sat on the edge of the bench seat and said little. Brynna kept urging her to drink and eat from time to time but she had no stomach for either. She prayed unceasingly for Eghan, wondering if he was alive or dead, and chided herself for not paying attention to the dread she had felt before leaving home. She should never have left. She should have stayed with her own people. Perhaps she could have done something ... she groaned aloud. She knew there was nothing she could have done to prevent what had happened in the Valley of Lhin. But what did happen, exactly? Eghan ... she groaned again, knowing how keenly he would feel the death of his father. She had to believe he was alive but wondered if anyone was with him. Was his new wife at his side? Had his guardian been killed as well? And what of Adlair? A pang of deep loss went through her and hot tears began seeping from her eyes again.

Brynna leaned forward to place a hand on her knee. "We will be home soon, my lady."

Nara tried to smile at her handmaid, but then remembered the face she had seen in the Brimleish court. Could it truly have been Eghan? If it was, then he was indeed alive and she was fleeing further and further away from him. Perhaps she should order the carriage to turn around. She sat back. No. That man could not have been Eghan. It was only a figment of her imagination, a wishful apparition or perhaps a premonition. She shivered. She must be within her own kingdom as quickly as possible. Even if Eghan were in danger, her first loyalty was to her own people. She must ensure they were safe, then she would pursue the truth about what was happening in the Valley of Lhin.

Brynna held out a cloth with bread and cheese. "Eat something, please, my lady, just a bite or two.

Nara took a few small nibbles, then sighed, closed her eyes and prayed.

They did not stop that first night, continuing on in the darkness, but as they prepared to head for the border with the Valley of Lhin the next day, Muirgheal advised that they travel only during the night. Nara tried to argue but he was insistent.

"It is not safe, my lady," he said. "And the horses need rest. There is an inn not far up the road. We will rest there, then continue once darkness falls."

"Very well." Nara sank back onto the carriage seat, too exhausted to mount much resistance.

Muirgheal began to turn away, then hesitated. "Perhaps it would be wise to send your men on ahead, my lady, to let your people know you are on your way. They can travel much more swiftly than the carriage."

Nara thought how Gage and Burke would be eagerly waiting for her to return so she agreed quickly but it took some convincing to make her guards obey her. In the end she won out and they charged off immediately with instructions to ride as swiftly as possible and report to General Gage as soon as they arrived.

The light rain that had been falling all through the night was letting up but it created a swirling fog that slipped through the dark trees and lay thickly in the ditches on the side of the road. Nara shivered and pulled her wrap tighter around her. By the time the carriage began to slow she felt as though the cold had drilled into her very bones. Brynna peered out the window as they heard an iron gate creak and then clang shut after the carriage rolled through it. Nara was too weary to respond when Brynna looked out and said, "What is this place?"

The carriage door opened and Muirgheal held out his hand to help them disembark. "A safe place for us all to rest," he said, and led them inside the building. Nara shivered again as she pulled the hood of her cloak back and peered down a dim hallway. The place did not offer any warmth. There was no sound of travelers gathered around a lit hearth, no sign of an inn-keeper or servants to attend them.

Muirgheal's hand tightened on her arm as she turned to ask him about it. He did not answer, nor look at her, but led her further down the poorly lit corridor. When Brynna cried out Nara tried to turn to her but Muirgheal's hand propelled her forward.

"Come, Queen Nara," he said, "do not resist me."

****

"Please, my lord, eat something." Latham held out the bowl of stew. Eghan did not take it.

"Just a bite, sir, to strengthen you."

"Leave me alone, Latham." He heard the boy sigh heavily but did not lift his head as he turned away, only pulled his cloak tighter around him and shivered. Would this wretched rain never stop? He stood and headed for the wagon. Ulhrik blocked his path.

"Balor will meet you here in the morning," he said, "to continue the reading."

Eghan did not look at him when he said the single word. "No."

When Ulhrik did not respond Eghan looked up. The old man's eyes were narrowed. "What has happened?"

Eghan tried to take a step around him but the old man blocked his way with his walking stick. "Tell me."

Eghan threw back the hood of his cloak. "Why does He torture me? What does He want from me?"

"You know what He wants, Eghan. Your heart, your soul, your mind. Stop resisting Him. You must offer yourself to Him, a living sacrifice as the scripture says. It is what he wants from all of us."

"I did that and He has repaid me with misery, taunting me at every turn."

"Taunting you?" Ulhrik's chin came up and he regarded Eghan with peircing eyes. "How so?"

Eghan turned away and almost groaned. "I saw her, Ulhrik, in the Brimladin court, on the arm of one who is whole and strong and ... worthy of her."

Ulhrik cocked his head. "The Alingan Queen? Here?"

"Yes."

"Are you certain?"

Eghan's voice dropped and his shoulders drooped. "I was as close to her as I am to you now."

"We must learn more of this."

Eghan pushed past him. "I do not wish to know more. I have seen enough." He climbed into the wagon, sighing when Ulhrik climbed in after him.

"I have a sense of dread, Eghan. We must learn more and quickly."

Eghan's head jerked up. "What do you mean, a sense of dread?"

Ulhrik squatted on the sleeping mat. "I do not know why, but I know we must learn what these Brimleish intend."

Eghan snorted. "They intend to have her married to the handsome prince who held her arm, to seal an alliance and gain access to the ore in their mines, no doubt." Eghan slumped down beside the old man. "And she would be wise to do so."

"Perhaps." Ulhrik pushed himself up. "I will speak to Balor. Someone may have gleaned some information while in their court."

Eghan held the canvas flap back and watched the old man hobble toward the gypsy's camp. Then he pulled back and wrapped himself in a blanket as he lay down. *Let him pursue it,* he thought. *It has nothing to do with me.*

He was almost asleep when Ulhrik returned, Latham and Isham in tow. Eghan was about to complain that they had woken him when he saw the look on Ulhrik's face.

"What is it?" he asked.

"Queen Nara left early in the morning, two days ago, with a Brimleish escort."

"So she is returning home. No doubt to prepare for her wedding. Why does that disturb you?"

"Because one of Balor's men overheard a soldier talking about their orders. Their route will not take the Queen back into Alinga Territory."

Eghan frowned and leaned forward. "Where then?"

Ulhrik shook his head. "I do not know. But I know we must follow them. And quickly."

Eghan took the pots Latham handed up to him, then leaped down and began helping them break camp. His thoughts swirled. Why would the Brimleish abduct Nara? Had she refused to comply with an alliance? But why would she? Or had the Brimleish decided an invasion was more to their benefit? *God,* Eghan prayed, *keep her safe.*

They had almost finished packing up the wagon when Balor arrived. Eghan had never seen him look so serious."Come with me," he said, whirling around without waiting for them to respond.

Eghan glanced at Ulhrik. The old man nodded and they followed after the gypsy leader. He led them to the edge of the camp where their horses were tied. Most were rather old, solid work horses similar to the one that pulled their own wagon. But Balor kept walking, often glancing over his shoulder and peering into the woods. He led them to another string of horses and these were no plodding animals.

Ulhrik stared. Balor gave him a sheepish grin. "The king's finest," he said.

Ulhrik did not respond.

Balor cocked his head. "You will never catch up to them with that old mule pulling that wagon."

Eghan moved toward the horses, selected one and untied it. He nodded to Balor and began to walk away. When Ulhrik did not move, he stopped and handed him the reins of the horse. "We will return them," he said. "Balor is right. We need animals with speed and stamina. Nara's life could be in danger."

Ulhrik took the reins. "We will take only two. Isham will remain here. The boy will ride with me."

Eghan nodded and chose another horse. It did not

take them long to pack and mount up. Eghan's mount pranced and he thrilled to the feel of a fine horse beneath him once again. Ulhrik called to Latham and the boy scurried back to the wagon, returning with a long shape wrapped in soft skins. When he handed it up, Eghan was even more thrilled to grasp the hilt of the sword of the House of Lhin and tie it firmly to his saddle.

Balor appeared at his side, his familiar grin in place once more. "I wish I could ride with you," he said. "It would give me great pleasure." He patted the horse's neck and sighed. "But I will guard your goods until you return."

He peered up at Eghan. "I expect you to resume the reading."

Eghan glanced at Ulhrik, then nodded. "I will," he said, "when I return."

"We have heard a rumor that a strange carriage guarded by soldiers stopped at an abandoned house some distance from the main road. Look for a split oak near the second bridge that crosses the river. You will see a little used road heading north. Follow it."

Eghan extended his hand. "Thank you, Balor. I hope someday to be able to reward you for all you have done for us."

"No need. Only return to us swiftly," Balor said. "God speed you on your way."

Chapter Ten

Nara was left in a small room with only a cot and a rough table as furnishings. She heard a bolt slide into place on the other side of the door and knew she was now a prisoner. She pulled back the heavy draperies on the single window but only a faint gray light streamed in. The casement was high and there was no hinge on the glass to afford escape.

Sitting on the cot, she pondered all that had happened in the past weeks at the castle of Brimladin Ula. She clenched her fists as she remembered the vague feelings she had tried to ignore, feelings that all was not as it seemed in that place. Had the friendliness of the king and his brothers all been a sham? And what of the queen mother and Talwynn? Were they just as duplicitous? Nara wanted to give them the benefit of the doubt but she was unsure. Her feelings had not served her well in these past days.

She stood and paced. What did this prince intend? Was he going to try and force their marriage? She would never agree. Or did he intend something more malicious? Nara wished she had not so quickly agreed to send her guards on ahead but at least they would arrive in Alinga Territory soon. She knew that when she did not soon follow they would know something was amiss and she knew Gage would be quick to mount a rescue.

She wondered what Muirgheal had done with Brynna. If they had harmed her ... Nara curled her fingers into fists again. If only she had paid attention to those pricks of unease. She shook herself. There was no point in that. She had to think what to do now. She must escape. She must find Brynna and get away. They would likely bring her food and water soon. Perhaps she could manage it then. God, she prayed, give me strength. Keep Brynna safe. Help us to get away from these men. Send help swiftly. Oh, Lord, she sighed. Help!

It was some time before the bolt rattled and the door squeaked open. Nara raised herself from the cot as a soldier entered carrying a small tray with a glass of water, a bowl of soup and a small piece of bread. She took a step toward him, her hands extended to receive it, grasped the edge of the tray with both hands, then flipped it toward the man, spraying him with the hot liquid. The glass shattered with a loud crash as it hit the stone floor. Nara whirled toward the door but the soldier recovered quickly, grabbing her arm before she could get more than a pace away.

Then Muirgheal was there, blocking her way. "Such attempts are futile, Queen Nara." His blue eyes flashed with anger. "This place is secure. The place where we are going, even more so. Resign yourself to this. You will be my guest for the foreseeable future."

Nara stared at him."What do you intend? What have you done with my handmaid?"

"Your girl is being held as you are. I felt it more expedient to separate you but she will not be harmed." His eyes narrowed. "If you are compliant." Glancing down at the shattered glass he growled at the soldier. "Clean this up and get out." The man hurried to obey. When he left the room Muirgheal took a stride toward Nara. She stepped back in alarm and he stopped.

"You will not be harmed, I promise you that," he said. "I am not a monster, Nara." The edge had left his voice. He leaned toward her. "I am sorry to have had to take this action, but my concern is for my kingdom. As we have seen, disaster lurks just around every bend. My people must be protected from it."

Nara believed he was sincere but when she stared into his eyes a chill went through her. "Your kingdom? Do you intend to usurp your brother's throne? Does he know that you have abducted me?"

"My brother does not yet see the urgency of our situation. When he does he will see the need for my actions."

"And if he does not?"

Muirgheal ignored the question. His eyes narrowed as he spoke, almost spitting the words at her. "All of this could have been avoided if you had agreed to marry me, or my brother. It can still end well if you will simply agree to a marriage now. If you prefer Brimwell, I will escort you back to him. The marriage can be performed immediately and then you can return to your home and secure the alliance by instructing your people to fashion the weapons we need."

"Never," Nara said. The word sounded more sure than she felt.

Muirgheal lifted his chin. "Then I will have to take other action to secure them. He spun on his heal and left the room.

Nara heard the bolt slide into place.

****

"We should keep to the woods," Jhonar said as he peered across a wide meadow. "There is a farm not far beyond this field. The man who owns it was a true and brave subject of King Gherin last time I met him. I believe his loyalties will not have changed."

The farmhouse was where Jhonar had described it. They stood in the shadows of the trees and watched as a small woman carrying a bucket made her way to a pump. There was no sign of the farmer. Approaching slowly, they kept as hidden as they could until they were within a leap of the woman. She gasped and dropped the bucket.

Adlair put both hands in the air, palms out. "We mean no harm."

She stared.

"We are friends of the true king, Eghan Lhin," Khalwyd said.

The woman straightened her shoulders. "Then you are welcome." She glanced over his shoulder, toward the woods. "My husband has gone to a neighboring farm but will return soon." She reached for the bucket. "Go inside. There have been soldiers about."

Khalwyd nodded to the others and they made their way into the small house. When the woman returned she went immediately to the stove.

"You must be hungry. We have plenty of eggs but no bacon." She glanced up. "Damon's men took our pigs some time ago."

Khalwyd was about to reply when the door burst open and a large man stood staring at them.

Adlair stepped forward. "We are ..."

"I know who you are," the farmer said. "The whole country is looking for you."

"Sit down, Harmon," the woman said. "I'm making eggs."

The man's eyes flicked to her, then back to Adlair. He dropped the bag slung over his shoulder and moved to the table, waving his hand for them to sit. He watched them intently but did not speak until they had finished eating.

"Your arrival here is well timed," he said. "There are a few of us, we are just farmers you understand -- but there are also many who have deserted Damon's army, more every day, who are joining with us. We are meeting tonight. We have decided to form a resistance."

Jhonar leaned forward. "Tell us what you are planning."

"We have no plan, yet, only the drive to put a stop to the terror that has gripped our land."

Adlair studied the man's face. "It will not be easy. There will be a grave cost to such actions."

"We have known peace and safety for generations in this valley. We refuse to forfeit that way of life. It is worth any cost. Easy or no, we will fight to get it back."

The man's wife placed steaming cups before them. "But what then, Harmon? With no king to lead us ..."

Khalwyd smiled at her. "That will be rectified, perhaps very soon."

Harmon cocked his head. "Are you certain the young prince is alive?"

Khalwyd nodded. "The prince is now your king. He was badly wounded but alive when he was taken away. We do not yet know where he has gone but we are depending on God's guidance to show us."

The farmer smiled at his wife. "Then perhaps we can help. We have heard rumors and now perhaps we can dare to believe they are true."

"Rumors?" Adlair cocked his head.

"That the young king has become a gypsy."

"Where did you hear this?"

"My cousin is a woodsman. He says he sometimes

encounters small bands of gypsies moving through on the edge of the valley from time to time. He says he came upon a group not long ago and there were those with them who were ... different. One was an old man. My cousin said he looked familiar."

Khalwyd glanced at Adlair.

"Ulhrik," Adlair said.

Khalwyd nodded. "Traveling with a band of gypsies would provide them good cover and safe passage out of the valley."

"Did your cousin say where these gypsies might be headed?" Adlair asked.

The farmer shrugged. "Who knows? But they go where they can make a living. The valley of Lhin is no longer hospitable for them. And Alinga Territory is not prosperous enough, so..."

"So the northern kingdom by the sea would be the logical answer," Jhonar finished for him.

The farmer shrugged again. "I have heard the markets there overflow with goods and silver. Good pickings for gypsies."

"But how will you find the king if he is in hiding?" The farmer's wife was frowning.

"We will find him with help from the One True God," Khalwyd said. "And find a way to restore him to the throne by His grace and mercy."

"What can we do to help?" Harmon asked.

"Do you have a wagon?"

The farmer nodded. "And a young mule that is strong and eager to pull it."

"We cannot pay you," Khalwyd said.

Harmon reached for his wife's hand. "Bring our king back to us. That will be payment enough."

The farmer offered to house them that night but they were eager to be away. It did not take long to ready the small wagon. Khalwyd's back throbbed and blood had oozed through his tunic. The farmer's wife had applied a salve that seemed to help but he was glad he would not have to walk any further that day.

When they were ready Jhonar stood back and nodded. "A little rough, but it will do," he said.

Khalwyd grasped the captain's hand firmly. "Be safe, my friend," he said.

Jhonar nodded. "And you, sir. I will pray you are able to find the king soon and return swiftly."

Khalwyd dropped his chin and leaned toward him. "Stir the loyalty of the people, Jhonar. We will need a strong and organized force to overwhelm Damon's men."

"And God's help in it all," Jhonar said.

Adlair put his hand on Jhonar's shoulder. "We know He is with us. May his will be done."

As Jhonar took a deep breath Khalwyd saw the doubt in his eyes.

"Could it be that it is his will that the Lhinian kingdom is laid low forever?" the captain asked.

"I will never believe that," Khalwyd said. "The fall of this kingdom was no doubt for a purpose, but I refuse to believe it cannot rise again."

"We must all have faith, both in God and in our young king," Adlair said.

Jhonar nodded. "I do." His chin came up. "In both."

Adlair climbed onto the wagon and took the reigns. Khalwyd heaved himself into the back, wincing a bit as he pulled himself up. He watched as Jhonar became smaller and smaller as the wagon lurched along a rutted road leading back into the forest.

Chapter Eleven

King Delmar paced from the large desk in his study to a long window facing the sea. He did not hear his mother enter the room until she spoke.

"Why are you so troubled, my son?" she asked.

Delmar did not turn to face her, but remained staring out the window. "Nothing to worry you, Mother."

He heard her footsteps as she approached, felt her hand on his arm. "Delmar." She said his name in that way that he could never resist.

He turned to her. "I fear Muirgheal is plotting something again, Mother."

"Plotting? Plotting what? What makes you say this?"

Delmar moved to his desk, lifted a sheet of parchment and held it out to her. "He has ordered our army to make themselves ready."

"Ready for what?" She sank down into a chair, her eyes widening as she scanned the paper. "Surely he is not planning a coup?"

Delmar shook his head. "No. At least, not yet. I believe he is planning an invasion."

The queen mother's eyebrows shot up and her

frown deepened. "Of the Alinga Territory?"
Delmar nodded. "Yes."
Aerwynna sighed. "Then his ambition and greed have ruled over honor and sense. What do you think he is planning?"
Delmar shrugged. "I have sent spies among his men to find out. It pains me to think I handed the Alingan Queen into his hands so easily. If he harms her ..."
"Muirgheal is misguided but he is no fool, Delmar and he does not have an evil heart, you know that. Surely he will understand the consequences of doing anything of that sort."
"I hope you are right. But if he thinks he can persuade me to support him in this endeavor he is gravely mistaken."
"And Brimwell? What of him? Is he aligned with his brother?"
"I have not yet spoken with him."
"Then that is our first point of action. They are close. Brimwell will likely know what Muirgheal intends."

The youngest prince stared at the floor as his brother questioned him. The king waved the parchment in the air. "What do you know of this, Brimwell?" he demanded.
The prince took a deep breath before he answered. "Not enough to be of any use to you."
Delmar sighed with frustration, but softened his voice. "This is no game, little brother. Muirgheal's

actions will have dire consequences, for all of us. If you have been in league with him in this ..."

"No!" Brimwell's head came up, then he dropped his eyes again. "I did suspect what he intended, but I swear, brother, I was not in agreement with what he was about to do."

"And what do you think he intends?" Aerwyna asked.

"To keep Queen Nara hidden and force the Alingans to hand over control of their mines. He said if they thought she was dead they would not have the heart to fight us, especially if we led them to believe the danger came from the Valley of Lhin and we offered protection."

Delmar slammed the parchment down on the desk. "And did he believe I would support such a plan?"

Brimwell nodded. "He believed that you would see the advantage and take it, in the end."

"And if I did not?"

Brimwell shrugged.

The queen mother stepped closer. "Does he intend a coup, Brimwell?"

"I ... I don't know." He looked at his brother. "I swear it, Delmar. But I do not believe he would come against you. His heart is not to rule, but only to protect our kingdom. He is convinced we are in grave danger and believes his actions are a way to prevent disaster." He hung his head. "I did try to dissuade him from taking Queen Nara."

Delmar was surprised at the harsh edge to Aerwyna's voice. "And where has he taken her?"

Brimwell shrugged. "To Caedfayr, I believe, though he did not say so directly."

"Of course," Delmar breathed a heavy sigh. "Caedfayr would be his choice - a fortress easily defended."

Brimwell nodded and looked into his eyes. "If need be."

Delmar whirled toward the door. "Then we will confront him there. We must try to put an end to this before it goes too far."

The queen mother stepped into his path and put a hand on his arm. She spoke softly to her son. "Perhaps it would be better to try and reason with him, Delmar. Coming against him will only make him respond in kind."

Delmar frowned but waited for her to continue.

"Let me go to him first," his mother said."Let me try to avoid a confrontation with the Alingans and any more of a rift between you than has already been created.

Delmar took in a long breath. "Very well. But I will not wait for him to ponder this. He must hand Queen Nara over to you immediately, or face me and the full consequences of his actions."

Aerwyna nodded. "I will make that plain."

****

Brynna flew into Nara's arms when they were brought out into the wet courtyard. Torches made shadows dance around them.

"Be strong, Brynna," Nara whispered in her ear.

Brynna pulled away and looked into her eyes, the questions and fear plain in them, but she gave a quick nod and looped her arm in Nara's when they were ordered into the carriage.

Nara heard Muirgheal give instructions for most of his men to go on ahead. She heard the word Caedfayr and wondered what that might be. A city perhaps, or an estate? She wished she knew, though it would make little difference. Wherever he was taking them, it would be their prison. They sat in silence, jostled by the rapid pace of the carriage as the darkness grew deeper and they rolled further away from the Alingan borders. Nara's mind was swirling with thoughts of escape but none of them seemed viable.

They had descended into a dark forest when Brynna began to pull her cloak from her shoulders. "Switch with me, my Lady."

Nara frowned. "What ..."

"We will create a ruse. I will leap from the carriage on this side with your cloak around me." She nodded toward the door beside her. "Wait a few seconds, then leap from that side, and run away."

Nara shook her head. "The carriage is moving too fast, Brynna. We'll be hurt. And I will not abandon you to these men."

The girl grasped Nara's arms. "You must escape,

my lady. We don't know what they plan but we know it is not good. We were only two days at most from our borders when we left the main road. But now we are moving further and further away into wilder and wilder country. We must act now, before we reach whatever place this evil man has set as our destination."

Nara peered into her earnest face, then looked out the window. The darkness was deep now, with no moon nor stars to soften it. She took a deep breath. Brynna was right. She pulled her cloak off and handed it to her handmaid.

Brynna pulled it on quickly and put her hand on the door. "I will try to follow you, if I can."

Nara placed a hand on the girl's. "No, you must go home, Brynna, no matter what. Go home as swiftly as you can and tell Gage what has happened. He will know what to do."

Brynna nodded. She squeezed her mistress's hand, then pushed the door open and leaped into the night.

Nara hesitated only a few seconds before doing the same, leaping from the other side of the carriage. She heard the shouts of Muirgheal's soldiers as she tumbled down a steep slope. She tried to grab hold of something to stop her descent but everything came away in her hands. Over and over she went, her body being battered by the rough ground, her arms flailing. Then suddenly she was in mid-air, falling into the darkness.

****

Eghan shifted in his saddle. They had found the house Balor Engre had described but it was dark and empty. Latham had pounded on the door but there was no response or even a sound from inside. Eghan's horse stamped impatiently on the wet stone in the courtyard as they circled it, peering at the ground. The rain had washed away any sign of a carriage but it was obvious many horses had been there recently.

"Where would they go?" he said aloud. His voice echoed back from the cold stone.

Ulhrik turned his horse's head back toward the gate. "Balor said this road leads west, into the mountains. That must be where he is taking her." He motioned for Latham to mount up behind him again. The boy looked at the door and opened his mouth to protest, but a word from Ulhrik and he leaped onto the horse again.

Eghan kicked his mount and it charged forward. The rain was letting up now. *A small mercy*, he thought. Perhaps they might eventually come upon tracks from the carriage, if indeed they still used one. He forced himself not to think of all the evil possibilities when he imagined Nara in the hands of men who were not honorable. Then he prayed, again.

Chapter Twelve

Ged tucked the blanket around the girl and sighed. "Where on this good earth have you come from little one?" he whispered. The girl opened her eyes and screamed. Ged leaped back and threw his hands up. "No harm," he cried, "I mean you no harm."

The girl stared at him, her eyes wide. He thought how rough he must look to her, an old man with a long gray beard, dressed in animal skins. He pulled his old felt hat off and tried to smile through his whiskers. Her eyes darted around the small room. The roughness of it too, might be a worry to her, he thought.

"You must be awful hungry," he said. He shuffled to the hearth and drew out a bowl of the soup he had prepared. He blew on it for a while before offering it to her. She sat up then, wincing a bit, he noticed, as she rubbed her leg. But she took the bowl and spooned it eagerly into her mouth. He smiled again. "My name is Ged," he said.

She spooned more soup into her mouth.

"And might I know your name, little Missy?"

The spoon stopped half way from the bowl to her lips and she frowned.

"I don't know," she replied, her eyes widening. "I don't know my name."

"Well, well now. You have quite a bad bump on your head."

Her hand went to the cloth bandage he had wrapped around the wound.

"Must have hit a rock when you tumbled into the ravine. You'll be fine in time, I'm sure, fine in time."

"Where am I?" The girl peered around the room again.

"In my humble home, child, in the middle of the Ferriston Woods. You are a long way from anywhere I'm afraid. But you are safe now."

When she did not respond, he cocked his head. "Do ye remember where ye came from?"

She shook her head and tears began to seep from her eyes.

Ged put his hands up and shook them. "Oh dear, now, oh dear, don't do that little princess, don't do that."

She sniffled but the tears stopped. "I'm sorry," she said, "But I don't remember. I don't remember anything at all."

Ged patted her hand gently. "Rest then, things will look brighter in the morning. The rain will stop, the sun will come out. Things always look better when the sun shines. You'll see, you'll see."

She leaned back and he tucked the blanket under her chin.

"Rest now," he repeated and pulled his chair from the hearth to sit by her side, humming softly to himself as she lay back and closed her eyes. "That's it," he said softly. "That's it, my little princess."

The rain did stop and the sun did come out, beaming through the small window of the cabin the next morning. Ged was proud of the quail's eggs he'd found the day before and was delighted when the girl was able to get out of bed to eat them, with the help of a wooden crutch he made for her. But she still seemed dazed, unable to tell him even her name.

"Well, then, I'll just call you Missy Princess. Is that all right?"

"But I don't think I am a princess."

Ged chuckled. "Perhaps not a real one, but one to me."

She smiled. "Thank you for the eggs. They were very good."

Ged smiled back at her as he took the bowl and placed it in the wash basin. When he turned back she was looking around the cabin.

"Have you lived here a long time, all alone?"

"Many years, yes. I had a wife but the fever took her not long after we were wed."

"No children?"

"No, no children. I'm just an old hermit, all alone."

She stared at her hands. "I wish I could remember who I am."

"Time heals, Missy Princess."

She leaped up suddenly, almost falling as she grabbed for the crutch. "But I don't have time."

"What?"

She frowned and hobbled across the small room.

"I don't know why but I ... I must go."

"Go where?"

Ged's heart almost broke as the tears poured from her eyes. She put her hands to her head and rocked back and forth.

"I don't know!"

He took a step toward her, wanting to take her in his arms but afraid to do so. Then she was suddenly there, clinging to him and weeping on his chest. He wrapped his arms around her. She was so tiny, so frail, so like the child he had always wanted. He patted her back. "There, there, Missy Princess, there, there. It will all be well in time. You'll see. It will all be well."

The next day she seemed brighter and able to move about without so much pain. In a few days she began doing some of the cooking and tried to set about cleaning his cabin, though the crutch hindered that process. He hoped she would continue it. Cleaning was something that hadn't been done in a very long time. One day she even offered to cut his hair and trim his beard. He thought she was settling down and he began to dream of the days ahead, of hot meals shared and afternoons sitting in the sun. But one day, after their noon meal, she asked him a question he did not like.

"Ged, how far is the nearest town?"

"Oh very far away, Missy Princess, very far and dangerous, too dangerous to travel through these woods. There's wolves, yes, wolves and other wild creatures."

"But I must go. I must find out who I am and where I come from."

Ged shook his head and patted her hand. "But not right away, Missy. You had a terrible tumble. You need to rest."

"My head has stopped hurting, Ged. I am no longer quite so dizzy and the bruises are already fading. My knee is still painful but I'm sure I could travel. Do you have a horse, or a wagon?"

Ged shook his head. "What need would I have for such things?" He stood up and took their bowls to the wash basin.

"Then I will have to walk," she said.

Ged turned back and nodded at the crutch. "But how will you make your way, Missy Princess? It would be foolish, so foolish, and not safe. Not safe at all."

The girl stifled a sob. "But I must. I must."

"Tomorrow," he said gently. "We'll talk of it tomorrow." He was relieved when she sighed but did not say anything more about leaving.

****

Muirgheal screamed his frustration into the woods. They had been searching for days but still had found no sign of the queen other than the scuffs where she had jumped from the carriage. It was as though she had leaped off the face of the earth. He paced, kicking at rocks and rotten logs. What should he do now? Go home and face his brother's wrath? He was certain that would put him in a dungeon cell. Carry on with his plan to enter Alinga Territory? He could still spread the rumor that their queen was dead at the hands of those who ruled the Valley of Lhin. The Alingans would have neither the heart nor the power to stand against even a small force of his men. They could walk in and take control without a whisper. He was sure of it. But what then? What would his brother do when he returned? Would he be willing to forgive him if he returned with wagons full of the much needed weapons he sought?

Muirgheal kicked at a rock that was more deeply embedded than he thought and cursed when the pain shot up his leg. His brother was such a shortsighted fool. Why couldn't he see their kingdom was in danger of being ripped away from them just as surely as the Valley of Lhin had been taken from its king?

A soldier approached. "Prince Muirgheal, the men are hungry and tired and night is coming on again."

"I don't care!" Muirgheal raged. "I want the queen found. No one will rest until she is found. Do you understand?"

"Yes, my lord. We will continue, sir, but perhaps it would be best if we could rest in descent beds for a night and be refreshed with a good meal, then continue in the morning."

Muirgheal was about to rage at him again, but thought better of it. The man was right. They could do little in the dark. "Tell them to mount up," he said. "We will ride on to Caedfayr and come back to continue the search in the morning."

The man bowed and Muirgheal mounted his horse. "Make sure that servant girl is secured. I don't want her disappearing as well." He charged on ahead, not waiting for the men to follow.

Chapter Thirteen

Brynna shivered when she saw the castle. It seemed to have grown out of the mountain, its walls carved from the rock, almost as though it were an extension of the mountain itself. Dark vines covered its walls and the wind whipped around it with a whistling howl. Her vision blurred suddenly and her head hurt terribly. She closed her eyes and prayed again that Queen Nara was safely on her way home and would soon send their soldiers to rescue her. She gripped her side and cried out as one of Muirgheal's men pulled her from her horse and dragged her toward the iron gates that barred the entrance to the fortress.

She almost fainted with relief when the man took her to the kitchens, not a dungeon cell. He shoved her down by a large stone hearth as a plump woman stood over her.

"Don't let 'er out of yer sight, Mags," the soldier said. "He'll have my hide if this one escapes."

The woman put her hands on her hips. "And what am I to do with her?"

"Put 'er to work or tie 'er in a corner. I don't care.

Just don't take yer eyes off 'er."

Brynna pulled her legs up, wrapped her arms around her knees and began to weep.

The plump woman clucked her tongue. "There, there, lass. I'll not hurt ye. Stand up now and let me look at ye."

Brynna obeyed, wincing at the pain in her side as she put a hand to her head.

"Are ye hurt?"

Brynna nodded, the tears seeping out of her eyes.

"Let me look at ye, then."

The woman pushed her hand away and looked at her forehead, then prodded Brynna's ribs. She cried out and jerked back but the woman continued.

"Don't think there's anything broke, just badly bruised likely." She peered into Brynna's face. "Ye've got a bad bump on yer head too." She scurried away and came back with a cool cloth. She wiped the blood away gently. "There now," she said. Ye'll be alright."

Brynna sat down again and sipped at the water the woman gave her.

"Who did this to ye, then? One o' them brutes?"

Brynna shook her head. "No. I ..." Brynna hesitated. Should she tell the woman the truth? "I leaped from a carriage," she said.

Mags cackled. "Well, that accounts for it, then. A foolish thing to do, don't ye think?"

Brynna did not answer.

Mags sighed and walked away. "Well, I've got work t'do." She cocked her head at Brynna. "Ever worked in a kitchen?" she asked.

Brynna nodded. "I can cook."

"Good. We'll get along fine, then." She turned away, but spoke over her shoulder. "But mark my words, try to run away and I'll have to call those soldiers to get after ye."

Brynna nodded. She did everything Mags told her to do, helping to prepare the meal for Muirgheal and his men. She was grateful that the cook allowed her to sit as she worked.

Mags was not happy about the men being there. "Never even a whisper that they was comin'," she grumbled. "And so many of 'em! What do they think, that I just waves a magic wand and food appears?"

Brynna was not sure if she was expected to answer so she kept quiet and just did as she was told while the woman babbled on. When the meal had been prepared and taken away they sat down to eat but Brynna only picked at her food. When she thought of Nara out in the dark and cold all alone the tears flowed once again. Mags noticed.

"Eat something, girl. You're warm and unharmed now."

"But my mistress is not."

Mags' eyebrows shot up. "Oh? A mistress is it?"

"He was bringing her here but she escaped."

Brynna looked up when Mags grunted.

"Always thought that one had a devious side to 'im." She frowned. "But it's not like the king to allow such foolishness."

Brynna looked at her. "Perhaps he wasn't aware what his brother was planning."

Mags snorted. "Most likely. And when he discovers it I can expect more of 'em on the doorstep." She sighed. "We'd best prepare, just in case."

"You think the king will send someone after him?" Brynna brightened with hope.

"Aye and that will mean more work for this old woman." She gave Brynna a small smile. "But at least I have two extra hands to help with it."

Brynna stood and moved swiftly around the table, falling on her knees beside the woman. "Please, please, let me go. I must get home and tell my people that their queen is in danger. Please, let me go."

Mags straightened. "Queen, you say? What queen?"

"Queen Nara of Alinga Territory."

Mags' mouth dropped open and she stood, pacing to the hearth and back.

"The Alingan Queen?" She stared at Brynna for a long moment. "My mother was Alingan," she said.

Brynna leaped up. "Then help me. Please, I must return. The Queen could be hurt or ... worse."

Mags paced again. Brynna opened her mouth to plead but the woman held up her hand. "Let me think," she said and sat back down.

It was Brynna's turn to pace and the time seemed to drag into hours. She gripped her side and put a hand to her head as it began to throb again, but said nothing more.

Finally Mags stood. "Though I've seldom been there I've always thought of Alinga Territory as home and I've always harbored an allegiance to its royal family. "If this sly prince has harmed the Alingan Queen I'll not stand by and keep any fealty to 'im, no matter what it means." Mags paced to the hearth again. "You cannot get far on foot." She grabbed Brynna's hands. "Listen to me carefully, child and do exactly as I say."

****

Brynna fell from the horse as it trotted toward the house where she had lived with her queen. The pain in her side was like a searing brand and her head pounded. She sensed the commotion of men around her and felt someone lift her, but she could not keep from slipping into unconsciousness.

She woke in a small room, the queen's doctor leaning over her. He turned immediately and spoke to someone at the door. "Tell them she has woken," he said, then helped her sit up and gave her some broth to drink.

Burke and Gage burst into the room, asking questions as they came. She swallowed another spoonful of the broth and told them all she knew. "I don't know if she is alive or dead, my lords." Tears began streaming down her face. "They were searching but they had not found her when I ran away, but I don't know for certain if ..."

Gage put a hand on her arm. "You are a brave lass, Brynna. Rest now. We will find the queen."

She was glad to sink back onto the pillows and do just that, though her heart ached. She fell asleep praying again for her mistress.

****

"We must go immediately," Gage said as they strode down the corridor. "And we must go in force."

"No."

Gage stopped and turned to him.

"We do not yet know the circumstances, Gage. To go in force might cause more harm than good. I will go, with a sizable troop. You must remain here and continue with the fortifications."

He nodded, though it was obvious he did not like it. He grasped Burke's arm. "Bring her home to us, Burke."

He gave a quick nod and carried on, barking orders as he went.

It did not take long for the troop to be mounted and ready. It should have taken three long days to get to the place Brynna described. They managed it in two.

Burke sat his horse and stared at the fortress. It looked impregnable. High on a cliff face, accessible only from one side. They could never hope to take it by force. Burke sighed and prayed that diplomacy would get him the information he needed. He was about to kick his horse forward when a rider approached.

"There is a carriage coming sir, with a large contingent of men escorting it."

Burke waved at his men. "Move aside," he said, just as a column of mounted soldiers came into view. They stopped when they saw them, then moved toward them more slowly.

When two of the soldiers approached, Burke dismounted.

"What is your business here?" one of the men barked.

"We are looking for Queen Nara of Alinga Territory. We have reason to believe she is being held in this fortress, against her will. Who are you, and what is your business here?"

One soldier leaned toward the other and he turned his horse and galloped back to the carriage. No one appeared, but the soldier raised his hand and beckoned them to come closer.

Burke handed the reins of his mount to one of his men and approached on foot. A soldier opened the carriage door and Burke climbed in. The woman who faced him was stunning but her face showed the strain of long and arduous travel. Or perhaps it was from something more. When she introduced herself Burke bowed.

"I too have come in search of Queen Nara." The woman frowned. "Why do you suspect foul play?"

Burke explained what Brynna had told them. He could tell from the woman's reaction that she knew nothing of Nara's escape. He was shocked when she leaned forward suddenly and put a hand on his arm.

"Please, allow me to go ahead of you and speak to my son. I am sure I can reason with him. If Queen Nara is there I promise you I will release her to you, unharmed, immediately. If she is not, then we will need all of our men, together, to search for her."

Burke hesitated, but agreed. "I will wait, but not for long."

Aerwynna gave a quick nod. "I will send word back to you."

Aerwynna found Muirgheal pacing the great hall. She dismissed her men and the servants, waiting for the doors to close before confronting her son. "What have you done?"

Muirgheal sank into a throne-like chair. "We can turn this to our advantage, Mother. We will tell them she was killed at the hands of their enemies. They will believe it and then we can take control of the Alingan mines."

"The Queen is dead?"

Muirgheal looked sheepish. "I don't know for certain, but we have searched the woods for days. There is no sign of her."

Aerwynna whirled and paced back and forth, shaking her head. "You foolish, foolish boy. You have gone too far this time, Muirgheal. You will be fortunate if Delmar does not lock you in the dungeons of Brimladin Ula. If this causes a war, he would be well within his right to have you hung."

Muirgheal stood up and fell to his knees at his mother's feet. "Please, Mother, appeal to him on my behalf. I only acted out of loyalty to our realm, out of fear that the kingdom would be snatched from us."

Aerwynna sighed. "I am inclined to let him deal with you as he will, Muirgheal, but you may be able to restore some of my faith in you if you do as I say."

He looked up and nodded.

"You will march out to those soldiers who are waiting beyond these gates and you will tell them what you have done. Then you will offer them any assistance they require in searching for their Queen."

"But ..."

"Do not defy me in this, Muirgheal. You will do it or I will have you put in chains immediately. Do you understand me?"

He dropped his head and nodded again.

Aerwynna grasped his arm and made him stand. "March!"

She held her breath and watched the man, Burke, intently. She knew he would be inclined to arrest her son, though he had just confessed to him with a humility she had never seen him exhibit before. But they all knew that would cause a clash with the soldiers gathered around them. She hoped he would let it go, at least for now. Nara's rescue was paramount. The queen mother stepped forward. Her son scuttled behind her.

"We will lead you to the place where she leaped from the coach and join your men in a thorough systematic search," she said.

Burke nodded and ordered his men to mount.

Chapter Fourteen

Eghan stroked his horse's muzzle and prayed it would stay quiet. A well-armed troop of soldiers trotted by, only a few feet from where they hid in the bushes. When the men were gone Ulhrik touched Eghan's arm and nodded for him to mount again. Soldiers were a good sign, Eghan thought. They must be close to the place where the Brimleish prince had taken Nara.

He kicked his horse, wishing they could move onto the road, but knowing they had to stay hidden. His mind filled with memories as they rode, memories of his days in his uncle's house where he and Nara had met and become friends. He knew it would never be possible for them to be more than that, but he knew now, more than ever, that Nara would always be an important part of his life. If she was alive. She had to be alive. He would not entertain any other possibility. They had ridden for several hours when Ulhrik suddenly halted and pointed.

Eghan peered through the bushes and dismounted then moved quietly forward, careful to stay in the shadow of the trees. The gates to the fortress were unguarded. The place looked deserted but it was hard to tell. He sensed Ulhrik behind him.

"Should we be bold and just walk up to the gate?" he asked the old man.

Ulhrik did not answer immediately. Eghan finally turned to him. "I see no other way to gain access." Ulhrik nodded. "I will go," he said, and hobbled forward.

Eghan sighed as he watched his slow progress, glad when the old man finally reached the gate, rattled it with both hands and called out. There was no response for some time, but then Latham pointed as a plump woman stomped toward Ulhrik, a large club in her hands. They could hear her words as she called out, stopping half way to the gate.

"What do ye want?"

"Just to rest my weary bones and a bit of bread and tea if you can spare it, lovely lady," Ulhrik responded.

"This is no hostelry." The woman said, but let the club fall to her side.

"Aye, I can see it is a fine castle," Ulhrik said. "But there is no other shelter for miles and this night will be cold I fear. Just a pallet by a hearth is good enough for this old vagabond. Be merciful, my lady, and God will reward you."

She frowned and seemed about to turn away, but then shuffled toward the gate, opening it just enough to let Ulhrik pass through. She peered toward the spot where Eghan and Latham hid, then locked the gate again and led Ulhrik toward a small door to the side of the fortress.

Ulhrik made straight for the hearth and held his hands out to the fire. "Thank you, my lady. You have saved this old man's life."

"Posh and nonsense and stop calling me your lady. It is plain I am not." She peered at him with narrowed eyes, her frown deepening. "And what are ye doin' way up here? What's yer game, eh?"

"Ulhrik turned and gave her his best toothless smile. "I see you are a discerning woman, and I won't lie to you. My friends and I are searching for a young girl. We have reason to believe she may be, or have been, here."

"Friends?" She took a step back. "What friends, then?"

"Only two," Ulhrik hurried to reassure her, "a young man with a useless arm and a small boy, who wait outside the gate. They are harmless, and no doubt shivering in their thin cloaks."

The woman snorted. "And I suppose they are in need of a mat and a scrap of bread as well?"

Ulhrik continued to smile.

She sighed, then handed Ulhrik a large key. "Let them in, then. I've stomped up those stairs enough for one day. I'll put the kettle on."

As she shuffled to her task he heard her mutter, "More goings on than has been for months. Strangers afoot, princes and queens and Lord knows who else."

Ulhrik wasted no time ushering Eghan and

Latham in. The woman scanned them from head to foot and seemed satisfied they were no threat.

Eghan opened his mouth but Ulhrik put a hand on his arm and spoke before he could.

"May I ask your name, good woman?"

"They calls me Mags," she said. "And yours?"

"I am Ulhrik. He waved his hands toward Eghan and Latham and said their names. “We thank you again for your hospitality."

"Such as it is," Mags said. "They've all gone and left me with little, but as you say the Good Lord rewards those who are merciful."

Ulhrik ignored Eghan's sign to get on with it and offered to pour the tea. They sat at a rough table while Mags took out a basket of eggs and a loaf of bread.

"May I inquire as to the owner of this fine fortress?" Ulhrik asked.

Mags raised her chin. "It is the holding of the queen mother, Aerwynna Ul. It is the oldest of the castles owned by the royal family of Brimladin."

"But the family does not live here?"

"No longer. They leaves me to tend to it and to them, when they unexpectedly arrive from time to time. There's a watchman who comes, regular, mind, to check on things," she said, with a look at Ulhrik to see how he reacted to that bit of information.

"And they have arrived unexpectedly, recently, have they?"

Mags cocked her head. "How would ye know

that?"

Ulhrik leaned forward and lowered his voice. "I have heard some foul business has been done."

Mags clucked her tongue. "Aye, but she put him right, she did."

"The queen mother?"

"Aye." She cackled. "Marched him right out there and made him beg, she did."

Eghan blurted, "Beg for what? And was there a young woman here, with dark hair?"

Mags turned her eyes on him. "No there was not." She stood abruptly and took a frying pan down from the wall.

Ulhrik held up his hand when her back was turned, signaling Eghan to be patient.

"That is very sad news," Ulhrik said.

Mags turned to him. "Sadness is it? Yes, there has been a lot of sadness in the world in recent days." She turned back to her pan.

Ulhrik put his hand on Eghan's shoulder when he started to rise from his chair. He put a cup of tea in his hands, leaned back and sipped from his own. Eghan sighed but sat back as well and raised the cup to his lips.

Mags said nothing more until they had finished eating. She watched Latham clear their bowls away and pour hot water into a basin to wash them, then she looked at Eghan. "You are strung as tight as a fox on the run, boy."

Eghan glanced at Ulhrik. "I am eager to find the girl I mentioned. The girl with dark hair, like a raven's wing."

"This girl, she means a great deal to you?"

Eghan nodded. "She does. Have you seen her?"

Mags shook her head. "No, but I have heard of her. To think the Alingan Queen might have been right here, under this roof. It makes me light headed, it does."

Eghan reached out and touched her hand. "Please, tell us what you know."

"That weasel of a prince," Mags glanced at Ulhrik. "He brought her handmaid here. Fit to be tied, she was, and battered a bit, poor child, so afraid and worried about her mistress she was."

"What did she tell you?"

"That her mistress was lost. That she feared perhaps she was even dead. Smart she was, to leap from the carriage like that, wearing her mistress's cloak." She chuckled. "Wish I could've seen his face when he realized she wasn't the Alingan queen."

"Nara escaped, then?"

"Aye. Leaped from the other door, the child told me, but oh, they hunted. My, did they hunt, for days, men in and men out, in and out. Kept me runnin' the whole time with calls for food and drink and more bedding and ..."

Eghan stood and paced. Ulhrik leaned toward Mags. "Do you know where this happened? Where they were searching?

"The ravine, they said. It is deep and wide and full of ravenous wolves." She shivered. "Poor thing probably met a fearful end."

"We must go." Eghan strode back to the table. "We must find her."
Ulhrik nodded. "We shall. In the morning. We can do nothing through the night."
Eghan groaned and slumped down in a chair.
Mags pushed herself up. "I'll find some blankets for ye. This stone is cold on the bones at night." She paused and reached out to pat Eghan's hand. "The good Lord knows all, young man. He knows."

****

Gage watched as Burke and the column of soldiers rode up to the house. They all looked haggard and weary. He scanned eagerly for some sign of their queen, but there was none. Standing in the doorway, he watched as Burke dismounted and shook his head, moving past him into the house without saying a word.
Gage followed, allowing his friend to remove his cloak and sword and sit to remove his boots before asking. "Well?"
"The Queen is gone, Gage." Burke dropped a boot to the floor, rested his elbows on his knees and put his head in his hands. "Gone."
"We must send more men, expand the search. We cannot give up, Burke."
He looked up. "We saw sign where she had leaped from the carriage. It looked like she tumbled over the edge of a steep slope into a ravine. We searched

the length and breadth of it and the woods beyond, for days. There was no sign of her." He looked away. "They say there are packs of vicious wolves in those woods, and she would have been hurt after that fall, perhaps mortally."

"But you saw no sign of an attack, no blood, no pieces of her clothing?"

Burke shook his head. "Nothing."

"Then we must continue to search. We must assume she is still alive until we have some kind of proof, Burke, something concrete to tell our people."

"There is nothing more to be told, Gage." He stood and wandered to a window. His shoulders slumped. "The queen is gone, that is all we know." He was silent for a time.

Gage waited, trying to reconcile this news in his mind, trying to find some solution to an impossible dilemma. Nara could not be dead. He refused to believe it.

Burke straightened and turned back to him. "We must plan what to do now. Damon's forces are already massing at our borders and there may be another danger, from the Brimleish."

Gage's cocked his head. "How so?"

"The prince's plan was to invade. We cannot discount the possibility that may still be on their king's agenda, though the queen mother has assured me it is not. They need our ore and our weaponry." He sank into a chair and gave a deep sigh. "We can be certain Damon will invade when he hears this news, knowing we are weak and without leadership."

Gage strode back to him. "Yes, so we must find a new leader, one who can rally the people and we must do so immediately."

"But who?" Burke raised his head. "There is no heir, no one even close to the queen's line who is able to lead."

Gage put his hand on Burke's shoulder. "You are the natural choice, my friend."

Burke stood and shook his head hard. "No. I would never usurp the throne."

"Not usurp, but act only as a regent, until ..." He sighed. "If you do not assume leadership others will try to, and we well know there are those who would not lead in a manner honoring to Queen Nara's legacy, nor in line with the commandments of the The One True God. We have lived under tyranny before. We cannot allow such men to take control again. The people know and trust you, Burke. I know our noblemen will agree that we should appoint you as regent, at once."

Burke pushed his hand through his hair and groaned. Gage knew his friend did not like what he had been told, but he hoped he would see it was their only option. He let out his breath when Burke nodded.

"Very well," he said, "but we must make it clear this is only a necessary and temporary measure, until the queen returns."

Gage gripped his arm. "I will make an announcement immediately, explaining that the queen is believed to be dead and that you will take leadership until such time as that is proved wrong."

Burke sighed but nodded again and gripped Gage's arm in return.

"The first order of business will be to solidify our alliance with the Brimleish," Gage continued. "We must avoid any trouble from that quarter. As I said, the queen mother has assured us of their allegiance. She sent one of their generals with me, in good faith. I suggest we make overtures to them at once, perhaps send some forged weapons back with him as a sign that we are willing to treat, in spite of what has happened."

"Yes, a good plan," Burke said. He strode away again and stood at the window for some time before saying quietly, "I should never have allowed her to leave. If only I had gone with her."

"This is not your fault, Burke. The guilt lies at the feet of the Brimleish prince."

"And what measures will be taken to bring that scoundrel to justice?"

"Queen Aerwynna has asked that we leave that in the hands of her son, King Delmar."

"His brother? Is he likely to punish him?"

"I am told he is a just man."

Burke snorted. "We shall see."

"Yes, but for now we must focus on defending our borders with the Lhinian realm. That is where the primary danger lies and we need King Delmar's help."

Burke nodded. "Send for that general," he said.

The people easily accepted Burke as regent, though they were deeply saddened and angry to hear that Nara was missing. He encouraged them to pour their sadness into working hard to prepare for the attack they all knew would come. The Brimleish forces were newly armed with weapons forged with Alingan ore and had joined with them in regular patrols. Some skirmishes with Damon's men had occurred but so far no serious breach of their borders had been reported.

Burke leaned in as Gage went head to head in conversation with a Brimleish general and a few of their soldiers. He was about to ask a question when they heard a commotion outside the door. Burke opened it to find a small woman wrestling with one of his men. "What is this disturbance?" he demanded.

The soldier did not release his grip on the woman's arm. "I told her she could not bother you, sir," he said, "but she will not listen."

Burke put up his hand. "Let her go."

He released her and she took a step forward, peering up at him boldly.

"I must speak with you, immediately."

The intensity in her eyes made Burke's spine tingle. He nodded and stepped aside for her to enter the room. Before he could ask what she wanted she began to speak.

"My name is Cressina and I have kept a secret for almost thirty years." Her eyes darted from Burke to the others staring at her.

Gage motioned to Burke and they both followed him past the soldiers into a small study. He waved the woman to a chair. She shook her head and paced, her head swiveling as she stared around the room before continuing.

"As I said, I have kept this secret, but I am now willing to reveal it, for the sake of this kingdom." She swayed slightly and Burke caught her arm as Gage placed a chair behind her. She sank onto it and took a deep breath.

"Some water, please," she said.

Gage rushed to bring it to her. She took several sips, then looked directly into Burke's eyes.

"I understand why you felt it necessary to become regent. But there is another way. There is another heir to the Alingan throne."

Chapter Fifteen

She lifted the pail of water from the stream and was about to return to the cabin when she heard a man's voice.

"Nara?"

She gasped and dropped the bucket, whirling around as memories flooded through her mind. Nara. That was her name. Her fear was overcome by the flash of joy that she knew it. She knew her name! The young man striding toward her looked familiar. She watched as he approached swiftly, his arms outstretched. At first she thought to run, but the look on his face made her hesitate. It was obvious he was overjoyed to see her. When he was only a few feet away she thought he might embrace her but he stopped short.

"Nara," he said again, the joy on his face replaced by a frown as he dropped his arms. "Are you alright?"

"Eghan? Is your name Eghan?"

His frown deepened and he cocked his head. "Yes. Yes, I am Eghan."

"And my name is Nara?"

"Yes."

Nara thought he was about to say something more but his hand suddenly slipped to the hilt of his sword and he took an aggressive stance as Ged ran up behind her.

"Who are you?" Ged asked as he pulled her behind him.

"Who are you?" Eghan countered, "And why have you been holding this woman?"

Another old man approached, panting as he leaned on his staff. A young boy was at his side, his eyes wide.

"Perhaps we should all go inside and sort this out amicably," the old man said.

Nara stepped out from behind Ged and stared from one to the other. Ged grasped her arm. "Go away," he said and began pulling her toward the house.

The one named Eghan was suddenly before them, his sword partially withdrawn from its scabbard. Nara reached out and took Ged's hand. "It's alright, Ged. These men know me. We must talk to them." Ged opened his mouth to speak, but then just gave her a pleading look. She glanced at Eghan again. “They know me, Ged.”

He grunted and gave a curt nod. Nara waved her hand and led them toward the cabin.

"Ged, will you make us some tea, please?" she asked as they entered the small room.

Scowling and mumbling to himself, Ged did as she asked, rattling the dishes as he worked.

Nara took a teapot from a shelf and waved her hand for the others to sit. "I'm afraid we only have two chairs, gentlemen."

The boy placed one near the hearth for the old man. The other, the one she now knew as Eghan, remained standing.

"How did you come to be here, Nara?" he asked.

"Found her," Ged said as he placed the kettle over the fire.

Eghan stared at him. "You found her?"

"I had fallen into the ravine," Nara said. "I think I must have wandered through the woods for some time until Ged found me, brought me here and took care of me. He has been very kind."

"But why did you not return home?"

"I do not know where or what that is. I have had no memory of my home. I did not even know my own name until you spoke it just now. I was planning to go to the nearest town to try and discover who I am, but ... well, for a time I was not able to travel, and then, well, I have been at peace here with Ged." She smiled at him, then peered at the old man sitting by the hearth. "Where have you come from?"

"Lately from Brimladin Ula," Ulhrik said.

Nara took a step back, feeling the color drain from her face as she shivered.

Eghan stepped forward and took her hand in his. "Don't be afraid," he said. "We are friends. You are safe with us."

Nara felt a thrill go through her at his touch. She let her breath out. "Yes, I believe you, but that name makes me afraid."

"We will explain why, my lady, but for now you must trust us," the old man said.

"I don't even know your name, sir."

The old man pushed himself to his feet and bowed. "I am Ulhrik, a poor stonemason from the Valley of Lhin. At your service my lady."

"We will protect you now," Eghan said.

"I am her protector." Ged stepped between them.

"And for that we owe you a great debt, sir," Ulhrik said. "You have rescued a queen."

Nara gasped. "A queen?"

"You are Queen Nara, of the Alinga Territory." Ged put his arm around her, his eyes twinkling and his smile broad. "See? I knew you were a princess." She peered up at him. "But ..." Nara shook her head. "That can't be."

Ulhrik spoke softly. "I assure you it is true, Nara. There is much we will explain but we must return you to your people as soon as possible. The urgency is great."

"No!" Ged stepped between them.

Nara put her hand on Ged's arm. "Don't, Ged. It's alright. This is a shock, but I feel in my heart this is true and right that I go with these men." She tugged on his arm and he turned to her. "You can come with us. I will take care of you now."

Ged shook his head. "Oh no, Missy Princess. I cannot leave my home. I have been a hermit too

long, too long. You go if you must, but I cannot."
The sorrow in his eyes broke her heart but she turned to Ulhrik and nodded. "I will go with you."
Ulhrik waved his stick. "Bring the horses, boy."
Latham sprang to obey.
Ged moved to the hearth and removed the steaming kettle. "Have a cup a' tea at least, before you go. I'll bundle some provisions for ye."
They were all quiet as they drank their tea and ate some bread and cheese while the old man bustled about the small cabin. Nara's heart beat fast. At last she would learn about her past and it seemed, a lot about her future. She peered sideways at the young man standing by the door. He stared at her often. He was so familiar and she felt totally safe with him here. More, she felt drawn to him. But who was he? Who was this Eghan?

****

Gage exchanged a look with Burke and frowned at the woman seated before them. "Explain yourself," he said. "How can you make such a claim?"
"Because I gave birth to him, in secret, twenty-seven years ago. I have kept him safely hidden all this time."
"And the father ...
"Was King Oswhain Alingar."
Gage gasped. "Impossible."
Cressina looked at him. Here eyes did not waver. "I assure you, by my son's very life, it is true." Her hand moved under the folds of her skirt and she

revealed a velvet bag. She reached into it and pulled out something wrapped in purple cloth. "The king told me if ever this day came that I should offer this as proof."

Gage took the gold medallion from her hands, his eyes wide. "His seal."

She nodded.

Gage's eyes narrowed. "You could have stolen this."

She cocked her head. "And how would a poor village woman gain access to the king's throne room? I assure you I did not steal it. It was given me by the king himself, when the troubles came upon us." She stared off for a moment. "I think he knew his kingdom was about to fall." She gave a deep sigh. "And there is this. She drew out another small pouch and spilled a few gold coins into her hand. "These are all that is left of the chest he buried behind my house before he left me. This gold he took from his own treasury has supplied us with all we have needed all these years. When it began to dwindle I knew the time was near for my son to make himself known. When I heard of Queen Nara's disappearance I knew for certain that time had come." She handed Gage a small parchment scroll. "And he left this, written in his own hand."

Gage unrolled the scroll, read it and sat down as though his legs had given out under him. He knew the king's hand had written it. He nodded at Burke. "It is authentic," he said.

Cressina took a deep breath. Gage saw the sadness

in her eyes when she looked at him again. "When you see my son you will believe what I have said. He is the image of his father. His name is Cedhrik and now that Queen Nara is dead, he is the sole heir to the Alingan throne."

Gage leaped up and took a step toward the old woman. "Take us to him," he said.

It took two days to arrive at the place. Cressina led them through the side streets of the small villages, avoiding the main squares where people had congregated for market. Then they entered a dark wood. The path the woman took was barely visible in the dim light. The house she led them to was tiny and well hidden but its yard was neat and clean. As they approached it they could hear the rhythmic whack of someone chopping wood.

When Gage rounded the corner of the house and saw the young man with the axe in his hand, he stopped in his tracks. He could only see the man from the back but his form was familiar. Memories of the king Gage once served poured into his mind like a soothing brook.

Cedhrik turned as his mother approached. He put the axe down and said calmly. "So, they believed you."

"Not entirely," his mother said, glancing at the two men staring at her son. "But when you remove the mask I believe they will."

The man reached up and lifted a leather sheild that hid most of his face.

Gage sucked in his breath. The man did not just resemble the long dead king, he looked like his twin. Gage fell to one knee. Burke did likewise.

The man gave a deep sigh. "Well then, I suppose I must go with you. Please, stand up."

Burke took a step forward, bowed and introduced himself. Then he turned to Gage and introduced him as a general he could trust. "We must act quickly," he said, "to establish your claim to the throne."

Cedhrik nodded. "I understand." He glanced at his mother and looked at the mask still in his hand. "I have known for some time that this day would come but I confess I am reluctant. And I am afraid I am ill prepared for it. I will need your guidance as well as your allegiance in the days to come."

Burke raised his chin and straightened. "You are, or soon will, be our king. You will have every support we are able to give."

Cedhrik nodded. "There are a few things I wish to take with me, and a few moments are needed to say good-bye to my mother."

"You may bring her with you," Burke said. "As your mother she will be provided with rooms in your house."

Cressina chuckled. "Me in a grand house?" She gave her son a slow sad smile.

Gage understood the sadness. Her son was no longer her own.

"No," she said. "This he must do alone."

Cedhrik nodded, left the mask on the chopping

block and moved past them into the house, the woman following.

Gage lifted the mask and sank down onto the stump. "This is like a dream." He stared at the door the two had just walked through.

"Or a nightmare." Burke paced. "He said himself he is not prepared to be a king. What if Nara is not dead? We have no real proof. What if she returns to find a usurper on the throne?"

"Then she will take her rightful place. Her claim is stronger than that of an illegitimate son."

Burke shook his head. "But what if this Cedhrik does not want to give up the throne once he has taken it? That could throw us into a civil war, one our kingdom would not survive."

"We could list all the 'what ifs' for hours, Burke," Gage said, "But for now, can you not see that he is a God-send? We can't deny he is the answer to our dilemma. We will have to school him a great deal, yes, but we have a leader now, and God willing, someone who can rally the people to defend Alinga Territory."

Burke sighed. "But we know nothing about him. What if he is entirely unsuitable? What if he is unable to reign as a king must?"

"Do you not see that he has the bearing of a king? He is his father's son. We will have to trust in that." Gage stared off as though remembering. "Seeing him ... it is like stepping back in time." He stood and gripped his friend's arm. "I believe God has a plan, Burke and I believe this young man will have a crucial role in it. We must trust in the One True God."

Burke nodded and sighed again. "God help us all."

Chapter Sixteen

Damon read the message a servant had just handed him and smiled. "Perfect," he said. He peered into the faces of his generals sitting at a large table.

"The Alingan Queen is assumed dead."

The men cheered, clapping one another on their backs as though they had won a great victory. Damon's smile became a smirk. "They will be demoralized at this news and when they see the numbers of our army, our black armor gleaming, they will faint with fear." He laughed. "And we will take what is rightfully ours with barely a fight."

One of the generals cleared his throat. "And what of the rebellion my lord? The rebels are continuing to cause havoc."

"Do you think I fear a few unarmed farmers and boys? Discover who they are. Crush them. See that they are publicly punished and executed and we will have no more rebellion to worry about. I expect it to be done immediately, do you hear? I'll no longer suffer these gnats about my ears."

"Yes, my lord."

"Well, why are you sitting there? Go!"

The soldier stood, bowed and left the chamber. The other generals leaned forward as Damon outlined his plan. When he was finished he studied the faces around the table. None of them made eye contact. Some were half turned away. All of them were frowning.

"What?" he demanded.

No one spoke for a few moments but when Damon continued to stare one of the generals faced him and took a deep breath. "Our numbers are, well, my lord, our numbers ..." The general's eyes darted around the table but no one met his gaze. Damon pounded the table. "What are you saying? Out with it!"

"There just aren't that many trained men in the ranks now, my lord," the soldier blurted. "At least, not as many as you have assumed. There have been many desertions, my lord. Mostly those once loyal to the House of Lhin, you understand. They have deserted and we assumed they had fled into the forests and mountains but some have been seen with these farmers. Some are trained fighters, my Lord. To attack on more than one front, as you have suggested ..." He shook his head. "I fear it would be foolhardy."

Another soldier cleared his throat and spread his hands on the table. "We know the Brimleish have joined with them and there have been rumors, my lord, that the Clansmen are on their way. If they are able to mount a strong force and reach the Alingan's camp in time, they may very well outnumber us significantly."

Damon whirled around and strode across the room. He remained at the high window for some time, staring out and mumbling to himself. The men jumped when he suddenly let out a loud cackle.

"Send the sorcerers to me immediately."

The generals rose, bowed and hurried from the room.

****

Jhonar looked at the faces gathered in the large barn. They were serious, some grim, but they were also eager.

"I won't lie to you," Jhonar began. "Some of you may die today. Some will be whipped and thrown into prison. Your families will suffer. But one day soon your king will return and when he does he will reward you, he will restore what has been taken from you and we will all once again live in peace and prosperity. So think about that day and take courage." He paused and scanned the faces.

"Damon means to rule with an iron fist and leave you and your families to starve. He means to destroy all that has been built in this kingdom in the past. I say we make his life more miserable than he makes ours. Are you with me?"

The crowd erupted with cheers. Jhonar saw the fists raised in the air, some of them holding pitchforks and clubs, and he nodded. "Then God be with us." He leaped down from the hay rack on which he stood and led the men outside.

He was confident of the plan. They did not stand a chance against Damon's forces by going against them in an all out battle, but they could worry them, cause constant irritations on several fronts at once, make them chase their tails morning and night. *Yes,* Jhonar thought, *there is more than one way to wage war*. He nodded to a man he had known as a loyal soldier in King Gherin's guard. Many of his own men had deserted Damon and joined this rag-tag bunch. Jhonar watched as they split off into small groups and headed in different directions. Then he turned to the farmer standing beside him. "You understand the plan?" he asked.

The man nodded and held up a small bag. "I've blown up enough tree stumps to know how this powder works. And they will never suspect a farmer would dare try to destroy an armory."

Jhonar clapped him on the back. "Be careful. If they catch you with that pouch they will know what you intend and they will not treat you gently. And remember the timing. At the stroke of noon, no sooner."

The man nodded and walked away. Jhonar signaled the six men waiting and they moved off in another direction. There were men in the dungeons who would fight bravely once released.

****

Khalwyd and Adlair lay flat on the top of a small rise. The gypsy camp was below them, six or seven wagons arranged in a wide circle beside a small lake. They watched for a time as a few women and children began to stir with the early morning light. Adlair tapped Khalwyd's arm and they squirmed their way back down the embankment.

"I will approach them alone," Adlair said. "They will be more willing to receive a single man than one traveling with another who looks like a soldier."

Khalwyd nodded. "I will be close by, should anything happen."

Adlair climbed into the small wagon and flicked the reins. They made a loud slap on the donkey's rump and it jerked forward. As it rumbled away, Adlair saw Khalwyd jog around the small knoll and head for the trees bordering the campsite. When the wagon was a few yards from it, Adlair pulled on the reins and waited. Within moments a tall man with braids and a bright red bandanna around his neck approached. Two others followed a few steps behind him. They were big men and Adlair noticed one of them kept his hand resting on the hilt of a knife tucked in his belt.

The man who appeared to be their leader stopped within a few feet of the wagon, scanned it and the surrounding area before speaking. Adlair climbed down and nodded to him.

"What is your business, traveler?" the gypsy asked.

Adlair decided to be forthright. "I am looking for

friends, three to be precise. An old man, a small boy and a youth with a limp arm."

The man's face remained stoic. "And what is your business with them?"

"As I said, they are friends, friends who are fleeing for their lives and may have looked for a safe haven among a company like yours."

The leader studied him for a moment. "And why do you seek them, exactly?"

"To restore them to their rightful place in this world."

"A quest to right a wrong, then."

"Exactly."

"Your name?"

"I am called Adlair."

The man's eyebrows twitched. "I know this name. The man who owns it is said to be a wizard of some power."

"I do have that reputation, yes."

"And your companion who watches us from the edge of the woods?"

Adlair smiled. "Khalwyd of Stohl, once guardian to Prince Eghan Lhin."

A look of surprise registered on the gypsy's face. "That prince is dead, so I have heard."

"What you have heard is only rumor."

The gypsy smiled. "So the prince you search for is now a king in exile."

It was Adlair's turn to show surprise. Again he decided to be forthright. He nodded. "Eghan Lhin is also my nephew, my sister's son, and I am very anxious to find him and restore him to the throne that has been usurped by a tyrant."

"I have heard what has happened in the Valley of Lhin at the hands of this tyrant. A shame to ruin such a prosperous kingdom."

The man raised his hand and Adlair noticed the two men behind him relaxed slightly. They stayed where they were as their leader approached and held out his hand. "I am Balor Engre," he said. "Do you have any wine in that wagon?"

Adlair shook his hand. "No, but I do have some good strong coffee."

"That will do."

Balor turned and led the way back to his camp. When they were seated around a fire he leaned forward. "Your candor may not be wise in this climate, Lord Adlair, but I thank you for it. It is unusual to meet a man who declares his intentions so openly."

"Urgency dictates the need for honesty, my friend, and I am led by One who knows."

"Those you seek are needed urgently?"

"Yes."

"Urgency often means trouble."

Adlair nodded. "There will be that."

"And if, perhaps, those you seek are not ready nor anxious to go with you?"

"Then I will persuade them."

"By what means?"

"I mean them no harm, but as I said the time is

ripe for action and the need for the true king to show himself is great."

Balor cocked his head. "I have heard rumors, rumors I do not like."

Adlair nodded. "Armies are massing. There will soon be war, perhaps on more than one front."

The gypsy sat back and sighed. "War is never good, but it can create a climate in which some can take a certain advantage, if they have certain information."

"True."

"If one were to commit to supplying such information, a prize might be acquired."

"You know where my friends have gone." Adlair held the gypsy's gaze.

"I do."

"Then I am eager to barter, information for information."

Balor sipped his coffee. "And perhaps a sack or two of this?"

Adlair smiled. "That could be arranged, if one might commit to keeping his eyes and ears open on other fronts."

Balor grinned. "A happy agreement, then." He stuck out his hand and Adlair shook it. Then he stood. "A queen has been abducted. Your friends, the young king in particular, was anxious to rescue her. I will draw you a map with directions to the place where they have gone to search."

Adlair stood and waved his hand for Khalwyd to join them. As he approached, Balor called for a skin to be brought and took a stick from the fire, drawing the map as he described where they should go. Then he looked at their wagon. "I gave them two fine horses. You will never catch up to them in that. I might be willing to trade for two good mounts, if the bartering is fair."

"We have little to trade, but considerations in the future could be of value to you."

"Then I will take your word on such and hope you and your friends are some day in a position to follow through on your promises."

Adlair nodded. "God willing."

He was surprised when Balor smiled and nodded. "Yes, God willing."

Chapter Seventeen

Nara leaned around Eghan's back as they trotted into the courtyard of a large house. She scanned it closely, hoping for some memory to slip into her mind, but there was none. They dismounted quickly and Eghan stepped to her side. He peered into her face, concern deep in his eyes. "Are you ready, Nara?"

She nodded. "Yes, I think so."

Ulhrik strode to the door and thumped it with his walking stick. A servant girl opened it. Her mouth dropped open when she saw Nara, she screeched and slammed it shut again. Ulhrik grunted and knocked again. Nara realized she was holding her breath when Eghan reached for her hand as they listened to scurrying footsteps behind the door. Then it flew wide. Burke burst into the courtyard and scooped Nara into his arms, laughing and crying at once.

"Oh my queen," he cried, "Oh my queen."

When he released her, Nara staggered and peered up at him. She had no idea who this man was.

Burke's smile faded and his eyebrows knit

together into a frown. "My lady?" He glanced at Eghan, then at Ulhrik, who stepped forward and put a hand on Burke's arm.

"We are all weary. May we enter?"

Burke stepped aside. "Of course," he said. "Of course." He waved them inside.

Nara had only taken a few steps when she was caught into another embrace. When the girl released her, weeping openly, Nara studied her. The girl's eyes were wide as she kept repeating, "You're alive, oh sweet Lord, you're alive, you're alive!"

Burke touched the servant girl's arm. "Take your mistress to her chambers, Brynna, and tend to her gently."

Brynna nodded and began to move away. When Nara hesitated, the girl took her hand and led her down a corridor and then up a short stairway. She heard the rumble of the men's deep voices as she went and knew they were likely talking about her. She realized having their queen return in such a state would be a great distress to them all. As the girl led her down a corridor, Nara knew which doorway they would enter and when she stepped into the room she felt that she should know the place but no distinct memories surfaced. She wandered around the room, touching things as she went.

The servant girl stood by the doorway for a while, watching her, then she approached slowly. "May I take your cloak, my lady?"

Nara began to remove it but the girl reached for the clasp and undid it herself.

"I will draw you a bath immediately my lady. You must be exhausted."

Nara nodded. "I haven't had a bath in a very long time I think."

Brynna cocked her head and tears sprang to her eyes. "I'll take good care of you now, my lady. There is nothing to fear. You're home now. "

Nara peered around the room. "Yes. I think I am." She smiled at the girl. "What was your name again?"

The girl's eyebrows flew up. "Brynna, my lady. My name is Brynna. Don't you remember me?"

"Brynna. Yes. I remember that name."

The girl smiled and gave a quick curtsy. "I'll bring a fresh nightdress for you. The bath will be ready soon. She reached out and took Nara's hand. "Come and sit by the window while I prepare it."

Nara let the girl lead her to the window seat and allowed her to arrange and plump the pillows around her. She sat back and closed her eyes when Brynna left. The sun was warm on her face and she had a feeling of wellbeing that she had not known in some time. When she opened her eyes she knew what she would see. The courtyard looked familiar with its rim of wild flowers, a grove of trees in a corner and the large pool at its center. She knew there were fish in that pool and a sudden memory came of sitting by it with the man called Burke. She sighed. Perhaps all the memories would return eventually. But how could she rule a kingdom and a people she hardly knew? How could she be a queen when she had no idea what was expected of her?

****

Burke paced the large room as Ulhrik and Eghan explained Nara's condition and where they had found her. From time to time he interrupted them to ask a question. Cedhrik sat silently in a large chair near the hearth. When the full story had been told Burke stared at the young king and waited. He had only known the man for a few weeks but had grown to like and respect him. He had already shown great wisdom as a leader and Burke prayed silently that God would give them all wisdom now in the decisions they must make.

Cedhrik stood and placed a foot on the hearth's ledge. He stirred the fire with a poker and stared into it for some time. The others watched and waited. Finally he stood erect and turned to them. "My sister's safety and comfort are my primary concern," he said. "Whatever is to happen now, I want you all to understand that."

Burke noticed the men's shoulders drop as they relaxed. The tension was gone. Cedhrik placed the poker on the grate and addressed Burke and Gage. "I suggest you gather all our trusted advisers immediately."

Burke noted it was a suggestion, not a command.

"Instruct them to begin with prayer," Cedhrik continued, "then discuss logically what is to be done. The decision as to who should rule will remain out of my hands. I will abide by the decision that is made by the council, trusting that they will follow God's guidance. I am willing and eager to remain your king if they should decide that Nara is not able. But I am also willing to step aside should they decide she should be reinstated. The people have not yet had time to know me well and Nara is loved by them, so there should be little dissension among them if Nara is chosen. If the lot falls to me, I will do my best to peacefully prevent any dissension."

He turned to Eghan and Ulhrik. "I am eager to meet my sister, as soon as she is sufficiently rested." He nodded to them and left the room.

Burke let out a deep sigh, then turned to Ulhrik. "I would ask that you be part of this council, Master Ulhrik."

"God will give us the answer, gentlemen," Ulhrik said. "We must wait on him in prayer."

Nara smoothed the front of her tunic and waited. Burke and Gage both seemed agitated, as though they had to do something that they thought they would regret. Eghan placed a hand on her shoulder and she leaned forward.

"Speak freely, my friends," she said, trying to set them all at ease.

"My lady," Burke began, then hesitated and glanced at Eghan, then at Ulhrik who stood by the window, his back to them. Burke cleared his throat and began again. "My Queen, there is someone you must meet. His name is Cedhrik. He is your brother."

"My brother?" Nara frowned and twisted round to look at Eghan. "But I was told I had no siblings."

"So it was thought, Nara," Eghan squeezed her shoulder as he spoke. "But we have now discovered that is not the case. You do indeed have a half-brother."

She faced Burke again as he began to speak.

"A male child was born to a woman in a small village some distance from here," Gage explained. "There is no doubt he is your father's illegitimate son."

Nara put a hand to her temple. "I have a brother?" She stared for a moment, then asked, "Where does he live? When will I meet him?"

"He is here, presiding over a meeting of your generals and councilors at this moment, in the great hall," Burke answered.

Nara stood. "Take me to him immediately, please."

Burke's eyes flicked to Eghan again.

Eghan placed a hand on her arm. "Nara, you must understand. Your brother has been ruling in your stead. He was crowned King some weeks ago."

Gage broke in. "Everyone thought you were dead, you understand, so when it was discovered there was another heir..."

Nara raised her hand to interrupt him. "I

understand," she said. "And have the people accepted him as their king?"

Burke nodded. "Yes, my lady, it seems they have."

Nara frowned. "But now that I have returned, alive, there is a conflict?"

"Potentially, yes. But a group of advisers have been meeting." Burke cleared his throat again. "At King ... at Cedhrik's command. He has acknowledged that you do have a prior and legal claim to the throne. They are meeting to decide if you should be reinstated and replace him."

"I see. Is he angry, then?"

"No, my queen, no," Gage reassured her. "He is anxious for God's will to be done. He is most anxious to meet you."

Nara let out her breath. She turned to where Ulhrik remained staring out the window. "Master Ulhrik? What say you about this?"

Ulhrik stepped to her side and bowed. "God's appointed one will be revealed, my lady."

Nara nodded and reached for Eghan's arm. "Take me to him," she said.

A page was about to announce them but Nara stopped him. "I wish to enter quietly," she whispered. The boy stepped back and bowed as he opened the door for them. They slipped inside and stood by the door. A tall man with dark hair bound behind his neck stood at a round table. There were maps and charts spread across it. One of the

Alingan generals was pointing out positions where their troops had been stationed. Cedhrik questioned him, leaning over the charts. Nara watched and listened for some time. Then she moved slowly forward.

One of the generals noticed and snapped to attention. Cedhrik turned.

Nara stopped and stared. She knew the lines of this man's face, knew the eyes, knew the slow smile that began to stretch across it. They were all so familiar as the memory of her father filled her mind. She swallowed and could not keep the tears from slipping down her cheeks. "Brother," she whispered.

Cedhrik strode toward her, took her hands and led her to a chair, kneeling at her feet. Tears were swelling in his eyes as well. He raised her hand to his lips and kissed it. "Sister," he said.

The generals backed away, leaving the two to speak alone. Eghan and the others remained by the door until Nara rose and motioned them to come close. She glanced at the table and the maps strewn across it, then looked up at Cedhrik. "Is there no way to avoid this war?" she asked.

Cedhrik shook his head. "It appears not. More troops have been deployed just this morning to resist an incursion of Damon's men across our borders. There have been several this week. They are getting bolder. I fear it is only a matter of time before they will come against us in force."

Nara looked at Gage, standing with Burke.

Somehow she knew this man was their military leader. "And are we ready?" she asked.

Gage stepped forward. "As ready as we can be, my lady. We have the help of several regiments of Brimleish soldiers. We have armed them well and together with our own army I believe we can withstand anything this Lord Damon sends against us."

"I have sent word to my friends, the Huntsmen who live in the mountains that border your land," Ulhrik said. "I am sure they will come to our aid as well."

"Good." Nara nodded.

She turned back to Burke. "And the advisers? Have they made a decision?

Burke shook his head. "No my lady. They wish to speak with you before moving forward.

Nara nodded. "Then we must do so immediately."

The interview took place that afternoon. Nara answered their questions as best she could and they were all encouraged that her memory seemed to be returning, more every day. But at the end of that time the group still could not agree on a decision. Some felt strongly that Nara was the rightful queen and should be reinstated. Others cautioned that in her condition she was not able to rule at such a crucial time and because the people had accepted Cedhrik as king they feared reversing that decision now could split the loyalties of the people at a time when their unity was vital.

When Nara learned that they were still in debate she asked to speak with them again. She asked that Eghan, Ulhrik and her brother attend.

"I thank you all for your kindness and respect," she said when they gathered. "My heart tells me I was, and am, greatly loved in this place." She smiled at Gage and Burke who sat with the advisers. "But my mind is slow to understand the needs and challenges as the queen of Alinga Territory. This is a pivotal and dangerous time in our history. Our realm is in jeopardy and firm decisions will need to be made in future days. I am not able to make those decisions as your queen."

There was a murmur from some of the men. Nara held up her hand. "I have met with my brother and I have prayed and I am satisfied that Cedhrik should remain king." Nara saw a look of relief spread over Eghan's face. Some of the advisors shifted in their seats. One of them opened his mouth to speak but Nara stood and her voice was strong.

"God is with us, my friends, and I have peace about this decision. I trust you will accept it willingly and give your whole-hearted support to King Cedhrik." She turned and faced Cedhrik and bowed before him.

Cedhrik strode toward Nara, took her hand and raised her up. "Long live Princess Nara," he said in a loud voice. The men stood to their feet and repeated the words in unison as they bowed before her.

As Nara and the others were about to leave the chamber Ulhrik spoke. "It is important that the people know you support your brother, Princess Nara. Perhaps an appearance together should be arranged?"

Nara nodded. "A wise decision. Burke, will you see to it?"

"With pleasure, my Quee ... my lady," he said.

They arrived together at the celebration. Nara smiled as they walked hand in hand to take their seats on the platform erected at the center of the city's main square. Music was struck and a young child approached Nara with a crown of daisies. Nara placed it on her head and laughed as the child clapped her hands and jumped up and down. Nara delighted in the festive atmosphere. The people seemed overjoyed that she had returned.

Cedhrik took her hand again. "It is plain the people love you, sister."

Nara smiled. "It would appear so, brother." She looked into his eyes. "And they will learn to love you, as their king." She squeezed his hand, then stood and moved to the edge of the platform. The music stopped and a hush fell. Nara smiled. "I am so very happy to be back among you."

The people cheered.

"I know you have heard rumors. Some of them have been exaggerated, I'm sure, so I am here to explain, and to ask a very important thing of you."

The people leaned forward.

"I have sustained a head injury that has affected my memory and my ability to reason clearly at times. These faculties are returning, slowly, but not quickly enough. I fear I am no longer able to rule as your queen."

There were mumbles of dissent. Nara raised her hand. "But God is good. He has revealed one who is more than able. He has given me a brother, whom I already love." She turned and smiled at Cedhrik, then turned back to address the people again. "God has given us all a king. I pledge my allegiance now, freely and without coercion, to my brother, King Cedhrik, and I ask that you do the same. Give him your loyalty and your love." She turned to her brother again and held out her hand.

He stood and joined her on the edge of the platform.

Nara took his hand and raised it high. "Long live King Cedhrik," she called out.

"Long live King Cedhrik," the people answered.

She nodded to the musicians and they struck their instruments. The people spontaneously cheered and began to dance.

Cedhrik leaned close. "Thank you, Nara."

Nara nodded. "God's blessing on you, Cedhrik, as a man and as a king."

Cedhrik's smile spread across his face. "Shall we dance?"

Nara laughed. "You will have to teach me."

"I'd be delighted," he said.

Chapter Eighteen

Eghan stood at the high window and stared down into the gardens below. Nara walked among the flower beds, bending now and then to pick a flower and place it into the basket her hand-maid carried. Emotion swelled up in him. It was all he could do to contain his joy when Nara announced in favor of her brother. Eghan loved her more than ever and now, perhaps, it would be possible for him to show that love, possible for them to be together. But should he propose such a thing? Should he wait until her mind and memory had been fully restored? Perhaps she would choose to be queen again. Should he deny her the opportunity to make that choice?

A sound at the door made him turn. Ulhrik entered. Eghan turned back to the window for a moment, then stepped away and sat in a chair by the hearth. Ulhrik approached.

"She is recovering well," Ulhrik said, glancing out the window.

Eghan did not respond.

"King Cedhrik asks for your presence at the

council of war."

Eghan shifted in his chair. "Why?"

Ulhrik snorted. "You are king of the valley of Lhin, Eghan. It is natural and proper that you be there."

Eghan stood and paced. "My situation has not changed, Ulhrik. I am a powerless king, a king in exile. What good will my presence do at such a council?"

"Do you have so little regard for what is happening to your people?"

Eghan turned on him. "I agonize over it."

"Then fight to change it, Eghan Lhin!"

"Fight? With this?" Eghan used his left hand to raise his right. "How can I?"

"There are more ways to do battle than with a sword in your hand." Ulhrik moved toward him. "You are needed, Eghan. You have met this Damon, you know his heart, how he reacts. All of that is valuable information now."

Eghan stared at him for a moment, then nodded. "Then I will do what I can," he said quietly.

Ulhrik put a hand on his shoulder as they strode from the room.

King Cedhrik acknowledged them immediately and welcomed them to the circle of men. "We are trying to discern where Damon is likely to attack in force," he explained. "It appears he is content, for now, with small skirmishes on several fronts, trying to wear us down. But I have no doubt he is massing a larger army to come against us. Can you give us any insight?"

Eghan picked up one of the charts on the table and sighed. "He is devious. He will do what you think is least likely, strike wherever he believes it will put terror in our hearts."

At that moment a soldier burst in, bowed and approached the table. "Your Majesty, My Lords, I have come from the border."

As he was about to say more another soldier entered, then another. Each reported the same thing. Three huge armies were massing on three different fronts.

King Cedhrik cleared a space for them at the table. "Show us," he said. The soldiers pointed out the places where the armies had crossed their borders.

One of the soldier's hands shook as he pointed. "The army I saw is enormous, Sire," he said. His eyes flicked to the other generals. "If there are as many ready to attack on two more fronts ..."

"God is with us," Cedhrik interrupted him, then pointed to each place, assigning his troops. He then turned to the Brimleish general who stood with them. "We will need as many men as you can give us, here," he said, pointing to the third spot on the map. The general nodded, assured him of their readiness and immediately followed after the others who had charged from the room.

"Do you have enough trained men?" Eghan asked as Cedhrik strapped a long sword to his side.

"We will soon know," the king answered. He

glanced at Ulhrik. "I ask that you both stay by my side, if you are willing."

Eghan nodded. "I can do little in battle, but I will do whatever I can."

Cedhrik gripped his arm and they strode from the room.

Eghan found Nara still in the garden. He did not waste time with pleasantries.

"The battle has begun, Nara. I am leaving for the front, with your brother."

Nara embraced him. "Come back to me," she whispered.

Eghan stepped away from her, then leaned forward, raised her chin and kissed her. Then he turned on his heel and hurried to meet the king.

He was impressed and rather surprised with the soldiers he saw massing in the courtyard and beyond. They were well armed, their horses obviously well trained. Cedhrik and the Brimleish had done their work well in the past weeks. Hope surged in him. Perhaps they had a chance at defeating Damon once and for all. Perhaps he would one day ride through the streets of his homeland in victory. If his people would have him.

Ulhrik was suddenly beside him and seemed to read his mind. "God willing," he said.

Eghan nodded. "God willing." His horse snorted as Cedhrik led the column out of the city.

****

Jhonar smiled as black smoke billowed from the other side of the city. As another explosion boomed he knew the entire armory was being set on fire. One of his former guardsmen tapped his shoulder. Jhonar turned to see a young boy lead the last of many horses away from one of Damon's stables. "We are ready, Captain," the man said. "All the horses are safely in our hands." It was a risky plan, using the young grooms and stable boys to slowly empty the stable, but it had worked. They had seemed delighted at the idea of causing grief to Damon and his men.

Jhonar nodded and another soldier raised his bow, the arrow's tip a ball of flame. His aim was true, the arrow flying through the opening into a high loft and landing in a pile of straw. They saw the flames leap up immediately. It took a few moments for anyone to notice and by the time the alarm was raised the fire had spread to the wall of the stable. In moments the whole building was engulfed. Damon's men were scrambling to organize themselves to put the fire out as Jhonar and his friends slipped away.

When the group joined the others the mood was high. The men laughed at the confusion and damage they had caused, slapping one another on their backs as they celebrated their victories.

Jhonar spoke quickly, urging them to speak to no-one about what they had done that day. "Go to your homes now," he said, "and spread the word to all who are loyal to the true king of the Valley of Lhin. Tell them we will suffer this Damon no longer. Our king is on his way and we will be ready to fight when he arrives. A new plan is already forming in my mind. I want every man and boy to assemble here tomorrow. Our work has just begun, my friends."

****

Damon raged when he heard the news. "I want them captured and punished. I want every man involved publicly whipped and then executed. Do you hear me?"

The soldier nodded. "Yes, my lord. We are searching for them, my lord, but ..."

"But what?"

"They are mostly just farmers and boys, my lord. There is no way to tell who was involved and who was not."

"Then arrest anyone. I don't care if they are guilty or not! Make an example of them. I want this rebellion crushed and I want it done now!"

The soldier avoided eye contact but nodded again and mumbled, "Yes, my lord." As he left the room a messenger arrived and lingered by the door. Damon waved him forward.

"Well, what of the preparations for invasion?" he demanded.

"Well, my lord," the messenger hesitated.

"Speak!" Damon commanded.

"The ranks are slim, my lord, and now ...

"What?" Damon almost spat at him. "Speak or I will cut your tongue from your worthless mouth."

"Now we are short of horses too." The man backed away, obviously afraid he would be struck. "But ... but the sorcerers are in place, my lord. They say they can do as you ask."

"They had better. Make sure they know their lives depend on their skill."

"Yes, my lord." The man bowed and turned to go.

"Have my horse saddled immediately," Damon called after him. "I want to observe our victory."

****

"There are so many," Eghan's voice was low.

They studied the long line of Damon's soldiers, their black and red armor gleaming, their horses standing still in the late afternoon light as the men pointed their lances and waited.

Eghan's horse pranced and snorted with impatience as he looked around him. Anyone could see they were badly outnumbered. Cedhrik had said nothing but looked worried as a general came to his side.

"Perhaps we should retreat, Sire?"

"No." Cedhrik raised his voice. "We will fight to the last man. This evil must be stopped. God be with us." He raised his sword and led the charge.

Eghan clutched his sword in his left hand and let the reins of his mount slip through his fingers as he charged forward with the rest.

Ulhrik rode up close beside him. "To the heights,"

he yelled.

Eghan frowned. He wanted to engage in the battle and Cedhrik had asked that they stay at his side. Why was the old man trying to pull him away now?

"With me," Ulhrik cried. "Guard my back! To the heights!"

Eghan groaned but turned his horse's head and followed. They halted their horses on a high ridge where they could see the entire battle raging below them. A line of Damon's men were engaged with Cedhrik's and it looked like they were pressing hard. A huge army stood behind them, ominously silent and strangely still.

"Why have you called me away?" Eghan asked. "I can still wield the sword of Lhin with my left hand."

Ulhrik did not answer but leaned forward, squinting. Eghan watched as his face suddenly split with a wide grin. "It is an illusion," he said.

"What?" Eghan sat straight in his saddle and stared where the old man pointed.

"The ranks behind the front line. They're an illusion!" Ulhrik stood up in his stirrups and raised his staff. "By the power of the Almighty One True God, I speak truth," he bellowed. His voice echoed out over the valley, making men's heads turn toward it. "Truth!" Ulhrik cried, swinging his staff back and forth. "Truth!"

Eghan gasped as the army behind the front lines began to dissolve in a swirl of black smoke. A roar sounded and the Alingans surged forward. Damon's forces, now obviously much fewer in number, began to retreat. The Alingans continued to press them. Eghan cheered as the line of black clad men were persistently pushed back. Large holes began to appear in their ranks. When it was obvious the battle had been won, Ulhrik cried out, "To the eastern front!"

They charged off together, heading for the battle raging in an adjoining valley. The same scene was repeated and they galloped off to the third front where Ulhrik's cry of "Truth! Truth!" affected the same result. It was there Eghan noticed a small contingent of Damon's men watching from a ridge opposite them. He saw Damon's standard and the gleam of his black and red breastplate. Then he saw the soldiers around that man suddenly flee in all directions. The standard fluttered from the heights like a wounded bird.

When it was over, King Cedhrik gave orders for his men to camp for the night and keep watch on all fronts. The men were energized by their victory but Ulhrik urged them to be vigilant. "Damon will have more than one trick up his sleeve," he warned.

Eghan tossed fitfully on his blankets. Twice he thought he heard a menacing hiss and raised himself. Hearing nothing but the sighing wind and snores of the men around him, he sank down again and fell into an uneasy sleep.

The hissing increased and became a sibilant voice. "Do you really believe your people will welcome you back after you ran like a coward and left them to suffer Damon's rule? They know you are not worthy of your father's throne. They know what you did. They will not want a tainted, maimed king. You will be disgraced before Nara and her brother, humiliated as you deserve to be. Slip away now, run back to the gypsy camp and seek refuge among them. They alone will welcome you."

Eghan moaned as the voice continued to hiss in his ear. "No," he murmured. "No!" He jerked awake and flung his blankets aside as he stood, his heart racing. He was about to go in search of some water when he heard a commotion and strode toward the sound.

A group of Alingan soldiers were marching two strangers through the camp, their torches crackling in the night air. Ulhrik came to his side as they approached. When Eghan saw who the men were he gave a yell and raced to meet them. He burst through the Alingans and embraced the two men. The soldiers fell back as Cedhrik spoke.

"So, what these men have said is true. They are friends?"

"More than friends," Eghan smiled. "This is my uncle, Lord Adlair, and my long-time guardian, Khalwyd of Stohl." He gripped Khal's arm. "I feared you were dead."

"If not for a certain captain of the guard I would have been." Khal grasped his neck and pulled him to his chest. "It is good to see you looking so well."

Eghan dropped his head. "But for this," he said as he stepped back, gripping his own useless arm.

"You have come from the Valley of Lhin?" Cedhrik asked.

"We have," Adlair said.

"Then we must talk. Anything we can learn of Damon and his army would be of help."

Khalwyd chuckled. "We saw what happened in the eastern valley. It seems you have it all well in hand."

"We cannot be too confident."

Adlair nodded. "We will tell you all we can. But some refreshment as we do so would be welcome."

Cedhrik ordered food and drink brought immediately. The men sat around the fires as Adlair and Khalwyd told them what they knew.

"Jhonar has organized as many as he was able to find. They are causing havoc among those still in Damon's ranks. I've heard even the cooks in his kitchens have deserted him. There are many whose true allegiance is still to the Lhinian throne. Their eyes have been opened over the past months and they realize they have been deceived. I believe many more will take up with Jhonar." He looked at Eghan. "And when they see their king returning to reclaim what was stolen from him, they will not hesitate to turn against the usurper."

Eghan nodded but dropped his eyes.

"This is good news," Cedhrik said. "I think it would be wise, then, to press our advantage now."

He paced before them, his brow furrowed in a frown. "I had thought to only keep our own Alingan borders secure, but now..." He addressed Khalwyd. "Can you get a message to your friends in the Valley of Lhin? If they are willing to join forces with us we will not just protect our borders, we will chase Damon's army to the gates of his own castle." He glanced at Eghan. "Or rather, to the gates of your castle."

Eghan nodded again but said nothing. The awkward silence lingered for a few moments until Khalwyd stood. "They are more than willing, they are eager," he said. "And yes, with a swift horse and God's protection I will get word to them."

Adlair turned to Eghan. "I have sent word to the Huntsmen. They should arrive soon, by dawn's light I expect, and they will fight hard at your side. When your people see you they will be energized to fight, Eghan. It is time to take back what is rightfully yours, and set your people free of this tyrant."

Eghan looked up, then dropped his eyes again. Again the silence was awkward.

Cedhrik broke it. "I would speak to King Eghan alone, my friends."

Eghan kept his eyes on his boots as they left.

Cedhrik sat beside him. "You fear a victory is not possible?"

Eghan shook his head. "No. The assessment is good, Cedhrik. Now is the time and I believe your victory is possible."

"Then why are you reluctant? And why call it my victory? It will be yours."

Eghan appreciated the man's forthrightness and decided to be as open in his answer. "I am not the able-bodied prince my people once knew. When they see ..."

"They will see only their king, Eghan Lhin. And they will fight for you and with you. Respect your people enough to give them that opportunity."

"But ... they will remember that I deserted them and ... and shamed them. They will remember when they see that their king is maimed. You can't know how they will react."

"I know they have been living under a despotic ruler. I know they will welcome his defeat. And I know a king rules with more than the strength of his arms."

Eghan sighed. "And what if I am no longer worthy to be their king?"

Cedhrik gripped Eghan's shoulder. "Do you think I felt worthy when they placed the crown on my head? I am an illegitimate son, Eghan, yet I believe God has chosen me for this time and this place. Go to Him. Ask Him for the strength to do what He has called you to do." He stood. “We attack at first light. With or without you.”

Chapter Nineteen

It did not take Khalwyd long to reach the border but getting across it without running into Damon's men would not be easy. He dismounted and crawled up a small ridge, making sure he kept below the horizon. Laying on his belly he peered into the rocky valley below. A small river cut through it. Khal could hear it burbling as it went.

There was a small group of tents near it but no men in sight. He was thankful that he had departed in the middle of the night. Arriving now, just as the sun was coming up, afforded him a window of opportunity to sneak through Damon's ranks and reach Jhonar's camp without being seen. He slid backwards down the rough slope, mounted again and pulled his hood up as he nudged his horse forward.

He was aware of the twinges of pain that still came from the scars on his back. If he were captured again ... He shook himself and he prayed that God would blind the eyes of Damon's soldiers.

A jolt of fear made him hesitate when he rounded the hill, but he pushed it away, prayed again, and urged his horse on, keeping the tents to his right and staying in the bushes until he was almost to the river. He made his horse stand for a moment, scanned the camp, then moved forward slowly. His horse shied at the fast running water, snorting and stomping. Khalwyd kicked its side and it jerked forward, leaping into the water with a loud splash. Khalwyd heard a shout and looked over his shoulder.

Damon's soldiers had been roused and were scrambling to their horses. Khal kicked his mount harder and the horse lunged into the middle of the stream, it's powerful legs surging forward, it's head up and ears back as it swam. They reached the other side and the animal seemed to know the urgency. He leaped up onto the bank and charged forward. Khal glanced back. The soldiers were still trying to mount. He squeezed his legs together and felt the power of the animal beneath him as it gave another surge forward. They were well within the protection of the woods before Damon's men had crossed the river.

Home, Khal thought. This was his land, the land he knew as well as he knew the lines of his own face. He guided his horse and slipped into a small draw that was almost completely hidden by bushes. He dismounted and went to the horse's head, putting his hand on its muzzle. The animal remained still and quiet as Damon's men charged past. Khalwyd waited for several moments before mounting again. He turned the horse's head into the draw. He knew where it would lead and he knew the farm where he had last seen Jhonar was not far away.

The farmhouse was quiet when he reached it. Khal watched for some time before approaching. He was leaning forward, trying to hear if there was any sound from inside when he felt the point of a sword on his back.

"Make a move and it will be yer last," a deep voice said.

Khalwyd stood erect and put his hands in the air. "I mean no harm," he said, turning slowly.

The man took a step back and cocked his head. "I think I know you. Are you loyal to Lord Damon?" Khalwyd hesitated. The man was not in any kind of uniform, but some of Damon's men weren't. Should he say yes or no? He took a deep breath and decided. "I am not," he said.

The man dropped his sword and smiled. "Well met, then."

Khal dropped his shoulders and let out his breath. "I am looking for Captain Jhonar."

The man jerked his head. "This way." He led Khalwyd into the woods where two others waited. The one holding the reins of Khal's mount was young. He looked vaguely familiar. One of the servants in King Gherin's stables perhaps. The boy's eyes went wide when he saw him. "Khalwyd of Stohl," he said. "Have you found the king?"

The other two men stared. Khalwyd nodded. "I have," he said and smiled. "He is preparing his return as we speak."

The men hooted and clapped one another on their shoulders. "Let's ride," the man with sword said. "Jhonar will want to hear such good news."

****

Eghan was dressing for the battle when he heard the tent flap rustle behind him. He turned, hoping to see Khalwyd. His mouth dropped open when Nara stepped in.

"Nara, what are you doing here?"

She smiled. "Do you think I would miss being part of your victory?"

He frowned. "It will not be mine, but Cedhrik's. And it is too dangerous for you here."

Nara cocked her head. "Eghan Lhin, have you too lost your memory? Have you forgotten the days when we went against Malnar in Alinga Territory? The memories that have been returning to me tell me I have lived with danger all my life. God has continued to protect me. I believe that will continue and his purposes will be accomplished."

Eghan dropped his eyes. When Nara stepped closer and touched his hand he pulled back.

"Eghan?" She asked, "What is it?"

He turned away from her. "How can you know His purposes are what we would want?"

Nara stepped around him, put a hand under his chin and raised his head so he was forced to look into her eyes. "If they are not, then what we want must not be for our benefit."

Eghan looked into her clear eyes. "I am not worthy of His purposes, Nara. I have failed Him, time and again, failed my own people, failed my father's legacy. I am not worthy of this victory nor any other. You don't know ..."

"Your worthiness has nothing to do with it, Eghan Lhin."

Nara's eyes cut him to the core with compassion but her words cut him more deeply still.

"Have you forgotten everything we learned in your uncle's house? The One True God is the only One who is worthy, yet he was willing to die for us all. We are His ambassadors, not because of what we have done, or haven't done, or what we are able to do, but because of our love for Him and His for us. We move and breathe and have our being only in Him. All else is vanity."

Eghan was quiet for a moment. He paced to the tent's opening and stared out. Men were rushing about, preparing for the battle. A soldier struggled with a horse in front of the tent, tugging on the reins as the animal reared up. The man stumbled back and fell into a large mud hole. The horse calmed down instantly, took a step toward the soldier and nuzzled his leg with its nose. Eghan grinned. *That's me,* he thought, *down in the mud.* He chuckled out loud as the horse nudged the man harder when he stood, almost throwing him off balance again.

Eghan heard him laugh as he grasped the horse's halter and leaned his forehead against the animal's. Then he stood tall and leaped onto the animal's back. It pranced but obeyed when the soldier made it back up, then move forward again. Muddied as he was, he was now once again where he was meant to be.

Eghan turned back to Nara. "Do you think He'll forgive my stubbornness and pride, yet again, Nara?"

Nara smiled. "You know He will."

Eghan nodded and held out his hand. "Then come, we need to find you a suitable mount."

When they rode up to Cedhrik he seemed surprised but smiled when he saw Nara. He nodded at Eghan and bellowed the order to move out. Khalwyd returned just as they were assembling, reporting that Jhonar's men were armed and ready to join the fight at their signal. Eghan was strengthened by his presence at his side.

Ulhrik rode up beside them. "This is an historic day," he said, "one that will be written down and remembered as part of the legacy of the House of Lhin and the people of Alinga Territory. I thank God that I have lived long enough to see it."

Eghan nodded. "I too thank God, Ulhrik, that He has not struck me down for my foolishness in the past. Whatever happens in the next hours, I will accept His will for my life. As flawed as I am, I

belong to Him and I will serve Him with my whole heart in the days ahead, if He will allow it."
Adlair's voice boomed from behind him. "God speed us to victory."

The mass of troops that flowed down into the valley stunned Eghan. The Brimleish were on their right, their drummers booming out a march that echoed through the valley. A troop of Huntsmen, rallying to Adlair's call, rode on their left. Eghan smiled when he saw old friends among them and urged his horse on at Cedhrik's side.

Ulhrik had insisted Nara move with him to high ground to observe but when they met with little resistance they joined the army again. They were deep into Lhinian territory before they encountered any significant numbers of Damon's men and most of those fled at the sight of them. Within hours they were staring down into the Valley of Lhin itself, at the castle Eghan had once called home. The windows were shuttered and the drawbridge drawn up tight.

Cedhrik sighed. "A seige would be unfortunate - long and costly." He glanced at Eghan. "Do you have any suggestions on the best way to breach this fortress?"

Ulhrik cackled and Eghan smiled. "I do," he said. "Allow me to pick a few men. We will enter the castle and open the doors for you."

Cedhrik's eyebrows rose. "You make it sound easy."

Eghan nodded. "With darkness and the element of total surprise on our side, it will be."

"Choose your men," Cedhrik said.

He selected only a dozen besides Khalwyd and Ulhrik. Cedhrik's eyebrows flew up again when he saw the old man among them. But when Eghan explained that the old stone carver had built a large portion of the fortress himself, the king simply nodded his agreement.

They rode down into the valley but kept themselves hidden in the forests until they were almost at the castle's walls. Then they dismounted and waited until the sun sank. Watch-fires glowed in the fortified towers, in all but the small one Eghan pointed out to the men. "Khalwyd and I will scale it and enter from above. The rest of you will follow Ulhrik and enter from below, through a tunnel that leads into the house of prayer. When you are assured it is safe, send a runner back to Cedhrik and lead a troop of our force to the tunnel. When Khal and I have reached the front gates we will signal for the rest to begin a frontal attack. Be as quiet as you can." He looked into Ulhrik's eyes. "God speed," he said.

He grasped Khal's arm and they trotted off through the woods, heading for the tower above the house of prayer where Eghan had once been imprisoned. He prayed the way of escape he had used had not been discovered and altered. He intended to enter the same way, by climbing up instead of down, using the notches Ulhrik had designed into the structure.

They crawled the last hundred yards. It was a slow and tedious pace but they reached the tower wall safely. The stone Eghan had pushed out those many months ago still lay at the base of the tower. He smiled. How good of them to leave it there as a marker and an aid to their ascent. Eghan tapped Khal's shoulder and his guardian cupped his hands. Eghan stepped into them, pressed himself against the stone and crawled up onto it, giving Khal his hand to help him scramble up after him. He went to the wall and felt along it. There! The first notch. He felt for another and pulled himself up. Notch by notch he began to climb.

It was a bit more awkward than he remembered, since he had only one hand now to pull himself up, but he managed. Khal followed. It seemed like an eon before they reached the open hole he and Latham had crawled through to make their escape. Eghan heaved himself through it and fell into the bed of straw on the inside. Khal followed right after him, wriggling with a grunt to get through but succeeding.

The door to the stairs stood open. They descended without sound, crossed the large hall of the house of prayer without seeing a single soldier and made straight for the front gate. Khalwyd took out the first group that came against them, almost by himself. Eghan was energized by his zeal and when several more of Damon's men came against them his sword flashed in his hand. They were within sight of the drawbridge when Khal shouted for him to release the chains that held it. Eghan fought his way through in short order. When the drawbridge began to descend the rest of Damon's men fled back into the castle. Khalwyd hooted and grinned at Eghan but he did not smile.

"Damon," he said, and charged after the men as the first of the Alingan troops flooded inside.

"We are overwhelmed, my lord. We must flee."

Eghan heard the man's loud voice as they burst into the room. Damon had already secured a chest of gold from the treasury and the men hefting it were heading for the other door. When they saw Eghan and Khalwyd they dropped the chest and ran.

"Protect me!" Damon screamed at the generals standing around him. "I will reward any who protect me."

Only two of the men followed his order and Khalwyd made short work of them. The others threw down their swords and fled. Damon cursed, ran to an open window and glanced down.

Eghan knew what he would see - the Alingan army flooding into the castle with little resistance. Khalwyd moved forward but Eghan placed a hand on his arm and raised his sword.

"Your day is done, Damon," he said. "Surrender and submit to the justice of the House of Lhin."

Damon sneered. "Never," he said as he leaped up onto the wide casement and looked down again. He turned and smirked at Eghan. "You will never humiliate me."

Khalwyd lunged for him but he was too late. They heard the heavy thud of his body when it struck the ground.

Chapter Twenty

Sweet smelling petals fluttered in the air, cast down from the windows and rooftops of the homes where freedom had returned. Eghan looked up and waved as he rode through the streets, Nara riding double behind him on a prancing white horse. Her laughter rang in his ears and she hugged his back.

Cedhrik leaned toward him from his mount to Eghan's left. "I told you so," he said, his smile wide.

Eghan fought back the emotion that threatened to choke him, thinking of his father and Silhas and all the others who had given their lives in the service of this kingdom.

They reached the doors of the castle and dismounted. A long line of soldiers stood at attention, eager to greet them here too. They passed between them, Eghan saluting Jhonar just before they entered. His heart soared as the doors to the great hall swung open and a chorus of trumpets sounded. The cheers of the people who were gathered there was deafening. Nara squeezed his hand. He bowed to her before leaping up the stairs to the dais. The scepter rested on the throne, waiting. Eghan stared at it for a moment, then turned and held up his hands to the people. The cheers swelled, then ceased.

"I thank you all," Eghan began, "and I thank our God for what He has done. This is His victory. This is His kingdom. Let us never forget the journey we have traveled to come to this place." He grasped the scepter in his hand and raised it high. "To the glory of the One True God!"

The people cheered again and it was some time before Eghan could be heard once more. "I want you to be aware of those who have helped bring us safely to this place." He nodded to Cedhrik and the Alingan king mounted the dais. Eghan grasped his arm and raised it. "King Cedhrik," he called out and the people roared. One by one he introduced his friends until the platform was crowded. When the applause was done Eghan motioned for them all to step down. Then he extended his hand to Nara. "And Princess Nara of the Alinga Territory." She beamed at him as she stepped up beside him. Eghan waved toward the tables laden with food at the back of the hall. "Celebrate!" he shouted. Music was struck and the people began to dance.

The next morning Eghan wandered through the castle. It had been swept clean of any sign of its previous tenants. Some things had been damaged and there were still dark scorches on some of the walls but that would soon be repaired. He took note of it all as he strode from room to room. When he entered his father's chambers he was surprised that it was exactly as he remembered it and the memory of standing over his father's lifeless body came flooding back. The pain of it throbbed in his chest but Eghan took a deep breath.

Then another memory filled his mind. He smiled as he remembered the look on his father's face as he told him that he had become a believer in the One True God. Eghan reached out and touched the post of the bed. "I will see you again," he whispered.

He went to the window and drew back the heavy drapery. A shaft of early light spread through the room. Eghan smiled again when he saw Nara in the garden below. He whirled around and hurried down to her but as he reached the edge of the garden he hesitated. He could see that her eyes were closed. He waited for a moment, then took a step forward.

Nara stood and smiled at him. "Good morning Your Majesty." She curtsied, her eyes dancing. Eghan cocked his head and grinned. "Are you mocking me?"

"No. You are the king and I am a guest here."

"I ... I would change that, if ..."

"If what?"

Eghan took her hand and led her back to the bench. He sat beside her and was suddenly tongue tied. "I ... I have longed for this day," he blurted.

"I know it must fill you with joy to be home."

"Yes, but that is not what I mean."

"Oh? What do you mean, then?"

He could see the teasing laughter in her eyes.

"I mean I have longed for the moment when I could ask you to be my wife but now that it is here I am not sure how to do it."

Nara laughed. "I think you just did."

Eghan was suddenly serious. "Then I have bungled it, haven't I? And I suppose I should have asked your brother first."

"I think he will forgive us if we do not follow the protocols in this."

Taking her hand again, Eghan slipped down onto his knees. "Princess Nara, will you marry this flawed and maimed king and make his joy complete?"

"Are you sure you want a wife whose mind is still somewhat rattled?"

"I am."

She smiled. "Then I will."

Eghan jumped up. "We will announce it immediately."

They heard a short squeal from the bushes behind them.

"Brynna, come out of there," Nara called.

The girl stepped out, her eyes downcast but a wide smile on her face.

"What do you think, my girl," Nara asked, "are you ready to help me plan my wedding?"

Brynna squealed again and clapped her hands. "Oh my yes, my lady, yes indeed."

Nara leaped up and they embraced.

Brynna took Nara's hand and began to lead her away. "We must leave for home immediately. There is so much to do, my lady, so much to do."

Eghan cleared his throat loudly. Nara turned back, went to him and kissed him. "I might be rather busy for the next while, my love."

"Must you leave immediately?"

She nodded. "It would be unseemly to remain in your house now."

Eghan sighed. "And I know your brother must return to his own throne as soon as possible, but can we set the date for the wedding? Say, in a month's time?"

Brynna was shaking her head but Nara nodded. "Yes, in a month's time."

Eghan wrapped his arm around her and kissed her again. "It will seem like forever."

Nara laughed. "You have much to do here. The days will fly."

The days did not fly for Eghan. Though he was busy making decisions to restore his kingdom to what it had been, the days seemed to stretch on and on. He kept runners busy with messages back and forth to Nara and Cedhrik until finally the day came for him to leave for Alinga Territory.

The wedding was held in the open courtyard of Nara's home. Burke and Gage stood on the platform. Adlair, Khalwyd and Ulhrik stood with Eghan. Even Latham had a part in it. Eghan grinned when he saw him with his hair slicked down and a bright tunic draped over his small shoulders. He seemed to be having a hard time standing still but Ulhrik's hand on his shoulder helped.

When the trumpets sounded and Cedhrik led his sister toward them, Eghan thought his heart would burst. For so long he had thought this day impossible yet here they were. Burke conducted the ceremony and as he began Eghan's eyes filled.

"God has done amazing things to bring these two people and these two kingdoms together," Burke said. "I think it is fitting to begin with prayer."

They bowed their heads as his voice boomed out. "Father in heaven, as we assemble here together in Your name, we are mindful of Your guidance that has brought us to this event, and mindful of the continuing need for Your Spirit's help in the days ahead. We turn therefore to You and in faith ask that You would not only be a part of this wedding ceremony, but also enhance the lives of these your servants, your ambassadors, in this their union."

Burke opened his eyes and smiled at Eghan and Nara. "The rings," he said. Brynna placed a ring in her mistress's hand. Latham took a moment to dig it out but stepped forward and handed one to Eghan. Burke led them in their vows as they pledged their lives to one another and slipped the rings on their fingers. Then he looked out at the people. "He who made them from the beginning made us male and female and said, 'for this reason a man shall leave his father and mother and be joined to his wife and the two shall become one. What therefore, God has joined together let no man put asunder.'"

Burke put his hand above their heads and beamed out at the assembly. "My friends, I present to you your King and Queen, Eghan and Nara of the House of Lhin, husband and wife."

The crowd burst into cheers as Eghan kissed his bride. They ran between a row of well wishers who showered them with rose petals as they dashed toward a shining carriage. But just as they were about to step into it, Eghan heard a familiar jangle of pots and pans. He laughed out loud when he saw the gypsy wagon approaching, pulled by two of Balor's best draft horses. The wagon was decorated with bright flowers and ribbons, its canvas pulled up on both sides.

The gypsy leader halted his horses before them, leaped down and bowed low. "May I escort you to your home, King Eghan?"

Eghan felt Nara squeeze his hand as he nodded. "Indeed you may, Balor Engre."

Balor led them to the back, attached a small ladder and bowed again as Eghan led his bride into the wagon. They waved to the people as it rolled out of the courtyard, the horses' hooves pounding the cobblestone in time to the shouts of "Long live the king! Long live the queen!"

The End

I hope you have enjoyed reading the Higher Ways series. I would love to hear your comments. You can contact me at smallpond@telus.net

You might also enjoy The Last Rite by M. C. Spencer, available soon on Amazon.

If you have enjoyed this book, please consider leaving a short review on Amazon.

Made in the USA
Columbia, SC
25 October 2017